Spirit Whispers

Finding Your True Calling in the Stillness

DAVID FABRICIUS

MVHL

SPIRIT WHISPERS
Finding Your True Calling in the Stillness

For permission requests, write to the publisher, addressed "Attention: Permissions Coordinator," carol@markvictorhansenlibrary.com

Quantity sales special discounts are available on quantity purchases by corporations, associations, and others. For details, contact the publisher at carol@markvictorhansenlibrary.com

Orders by U.S. trade bookstores and wholesalers. Email: carol@markvictorhansenlibrary.com

Creative contribution by Jeff Phillips and Mike Valentino
Illustrations by Matt Phillips
Cover design and book layout by DBree

Manufactured and printed in the United States of America distributed globally by markvictorhansenlibrary.com

New York | Los Angeles | London | Sydney

ISBN: 979-8-88581-204-7 Hardback
ISBN: 979-8-88581-205-4 Paperback
ISBN: 979-8-88581-206-1 eBook
Library of Congress Control Number: 2025903019

Contents

Acknowledgments

"David Fabricius is masterful at guiding people to the discovery, embodiment, and fulfillment of their higher purpose in practical and simplified ways.

"He parachutes into the desert in The Valley of Death—naked—and comes out leading lions. He inspires action. He is a capable, proficient, rugged, elegant, and wise infusion of Indiana Jones and James Bond with the heart of Gandhi. If you want a next level performance edge in every vital area of business and life, David is the right mentor and coach for you."

– Konrad Sopielnikow
Founder of 5 Enterprises w/ $2B+ AUM

"What is your personal "Impossible Vision?" Let David Fabricius show you a seven-step path to making it happen now. Spirit Whispers will inspire you to love deeply, live a more purpose-focused life, and contribute greatly. Do it now! David's gifting in coaching and leadership surpasses all others in practical application. David is globally known for helping successful leaders, business owners and managers become even more successful in unifying and inspiring winning teams for next level excellence, profit breakthroughs, greatness and societal contributions, making the world a better place for all!"

– Dr. Jennifer E. Herrera (Dr. J.)
Founder of AGE - Academy of Global Empowerment,
Business Education Expert

Foreword

Surviving five near death experiences changes a man and shapes his heart and soul. You're about to read the soul-capturing story of a man who has something very important to say.

I met David through a good friend, and I've been captivated by his experience and wisdom since that first meeting. His impact on me is something that is shared by thousands of others who have heard him train and speak in over 146 countries around the world.

When David was drowning while white water kayaking in Austria, God gave him a second shot at life. He heard God ask him four clear questions. These questions apply to each of us and immediately cause you to think about your life and all its values.

- What is my soul's destiny?
- Did I give love and receive love?
- Did I fully energize in life and my experience and feel the full flavor of life?
- Did I contribute and leave humanity and the world a better place?

David took this guidance from God and uses these legacy questions for his own life and for so many others as a North Star to living and inspiring others to live, a happy and fulfilled life.

David says, If you know that you lived well, then you can die well.

As a gifted spellbinder with his soul-captivating words, experience, and strong presence, David can transform an audience right in front of your eyes. The first time I heard him speak to a large audience in Las Vegas, Nevada, he mesmerized the crowd and yours truly. I have literally been to thousands of lectures, and David is one of a kind. He is a rare human treasure who captivates listeners with his intriguing life-journey that comes off like an Indiana Jones story on steroids. Subtly and poetically, he invites the audience into his stage performance and stabs your spirit alive making one want to fulfill their individual and collective destinies at a higher, better, and more profound level.

I predict that my friend David will influence generations of thinkers, readers, and leaders to live a life full of action, vitality, and yes—even spiritual fulfillment. As you indulge in this reading journey, prepare to hear your own soul whisper and yearn to be, do, and have more than you ever imagined you could. His amazing story shows you just how a caterpillar transforms into a butterfly, and how sometimes the butterfly needs to return to the chrysalis to be reborn anew.

This rugged mystery man causes people to vicariously wonder—as he speaks and writes—if they would find the courage to embark on a desert sojourn like he did, trusting the Universe to provide for their every need in miraculous ways, as he has done.

David's life has been a romantic adventure with all its twists and turns, giving him unique authority and credibility. He is the modern-day man on a hero's journey, with Providence granting him the nine lives of a cat. Like the book *The Alchemist*, by Paulo Coelho, David weaves

the must-read story of everyone wanting to overcome their pain and suffering and fulfill their unique destiny. I am certain as you read this book, you will see your story from an exciting new perspective and recognize your own hero's journey. May my great friend David's story inspire your soul to become all you can be.

— Mark Victor Hansen

Dedication

This book is dedicated to my late mother and father,
Mary Magdalene and William D. Fabricius.

I love you.

Special Thanks

Glory and All Praise to God for His Mercy on this sinner and for all my Bountiful Blessings. God is Good!

My deep gratitude to my mentor, Mark Victor Hansen, his beloved Crystal Dwyer Hansen, and to his Team—specifically to Carol McManus and the rest of the amazing Team at Mark Victor Hansen Library for seeing the true me and creating this book in world class excellence for me so that we may help millions of people globally through it.

A very big thank you to Maria who believed in the vision of this book, to Eric The Great, Ryan, Dr. J, and Dr. Glenn, who invested to make it a reality, and to Dr. Lisa for her help.

I am forever grateful. Thank You.

My lifelong appreciation to Mark of The Desert, for sincere friendship and brotherhood.

Onward and Upward – Together

A Prayer of Affirmation

Thank You for loving me.

Thank You for your mercy, forgiveness and grace.

Thank You for all I have.

Thank You for your Earth Angels helping me right now.

*Thank You for blessing my life with love, wellness,
and abundance.*

Please use me with purpose in the lives of others.

That I might use my gifts to bless others.

Prologue
The Rejected Barefoot Boy

Six-year-old Stig stood with his mother watching his dad walk with a very tiny suitcase down the long garden path to the front gate of their home.

"Mom, where is Daddy going?" She sighed. "On a long train ride."

"But when is Daddy coming home?"

His mother grabbed his hand firmly, pulling him in the opposite direction.

"Never."

Never seemed like a really long time.

As the years went by, the boy was sustained by the belief that his dad's dream of traveling the world meant so much to him, he had to leave those he loved. Instead of letting that destroy him, Stig held it in his heart as the ultimate quest for a man.

Stig's mother had only two years of education, and she struggled to support them. The two lived in a small village with four buildings in total. Stig ran barefoot as a child, never owning a pair of shoes until twelve years of age.

He remembered moving to a bigger town with four traffic lights, but it was 100 miles away from the first town where he was born—where he last saw his father.

His mother was a very beautiful, hardworking woman with great common sense. She often said the only reason that Rome was not built in a day was because she was not married to Caesar. Her grit and tenacity helped her become very successful outside of their small village in Africa; she became known for fashion as far away as Europe.

As a young teen, Stig was ill for a brief time with what he still believes to this day was misdiagnosed as a heart condition. In school, this resulted in him being placed in classes officially known as the "sick, lame, and lazy squad." He was viciously caned daily and assigned to pulling out weeds in the schoolyard while the so-called healthy boys played rugby. He was a social outcast.

This created acute discontentment in the boy, and he harbored a rebellious spirit of revolting against authority. In school, he was the ultimate underperformer and showed up simply because it was a legal requirement.

But Stig wanted more, and he knew in his heart he was capable of more. He vowed to prove that he was not sick, lame, or lazy. Outside of school, he visited the local village library almost daily, becoming a voracious reader and a dedicated student of stoic wisdom and life.

With his brand of managing his own education, Stig became self-reliant even while isolated. He was banned from participating in rugby and did not do well

in the marksmanship program or drill squad. Outside of school, he took up boxing, wrestling, and karate. As time went on and he matured, he excelled in boxing, and even more in karate, going on to win numerous medals in state and national championships.

His independence and lust for knowledge and self-worth, led to opening his own very profitable karate school and becoming a highly popular Sunday school teacher. He was a young man motivated by more than just building wealth which others measured as their success. He was determined to become a high achiever and to pursue a life of purpose and meaning.

Despite his "sick, lame, and lazy" status, every afternoon he would go for a hard run in the African wilderness that extended beyond the edge of the town where he lived. Barefoot and wearing only shorts, he set off, always carrying a large axe. On these runs, he would routinely chop a large log and carry it on his shoulders while running up a long, steep hill.

The combination of physical conditioning and the hot African sun shaped him into a vibrantly healthy, strong, young athlete with a Spartan-like attitude.

In his final year of school, he dated the most beautiful girl, wore the cleanest shoes, and drove a beautiful two-seater sports car.

At age eighteen, he was drafted, moving through various organizations within the Armed Forces. Each time he qualified for and gained recognition and notoriety as an excellent instructor.

At age twenty-two, Stig volunteered for Army Special Forces training. He passed the assessment and selection program and went through the one year of "operator" training under the watchful eye of one of the two most highly decorated for valor officers in his Unit. He admired and befriended both officers and Stig was proud to be one of only seventeen men still standing at the end of this cycle out of hundreds who started.

Only six were chosen for the reconnaissance and combat teams. Stig was ordered to go to a Special Forces instructor training program, where he earned first place out of thirteen students. The other twelve were highly-decorated, battle-hardened war fighters—men among men. In his opinion they were far greater men than him.

Stig enjoyed instructing new young volunteers in how to shoot, move, and communicate the special forces way. The abuse he suffered as a child and the need to overcompensate to survive in his early teens gave Stig an unusual blend of compassion and fierce physical discipline. It all contributed to making him an exceptional mentor and leader.

His next advancement was qualifying for and joining a very small, elite national counter-terrorism unit specializing in hostage rescue and later in VIP protection as well as limited high-value target arrest and capture.

Again, he was required to go through boot camp

"operator" training, as well as additional training in hostage rescue, VIP protection, and bomb disposal. This was despite the fact he was already highly trained in demolitions, military parachuting, direct action, and many other military skills.

Once again, he quickly became an instructor as that was a role that suited him well. He was appointed as a team leader, but due to the highly specialized nature of this group's work, missions were quite rare. Their days were primarily spent training and waiting for activation. By age twenty-five, he felt a burning ambition to pursue new challenges in civilian life. The transition from the armed forces (a place he called home for the prior seven years) to civilian life was not easy. With his experience, he was accustomed to high-quality leadership. Working for a civilian manager was not an easy thing to do. He was used to extremely high standards and an extraordinary level of leadership excellence in Special Operations. He found those qualities to be lacking in civilian organizations.

By age thirty-one, after graduating from The School of Business Leadership, he went to work for a prestigious multinational corporation. Initially, he was in charge of the security team at the corporate head office, then worked as a junior manager responsible for five cost centers. Toward the end, he worked exclusively on special projects directly reporting to the Chairman, before his career at that company ended.

Stig saw this as an opportunity to take his God-given talent and the unique character-shaping experiences life had provided and parlay that into the world of public speaking, inspiring and training others to a whole new level.

* * *

Stig is making an international name for himself as a dynamic and inspirational speaker, a world-famous sales trainer, and a fire-walk team building facilitator where he unifies teams and facilitates breakthroughs to uncommon next-level results.

He is popular with the world's most elite business organizations and top brands across six continents.

The subconscious drive within remains ever present to prove that he is not (nor ever was) "sick, lame, or lazy." By the time Stig reached his late 30s and early 40s, he was married, lived in a beautiful and opulent Italian-style villa, owned his first Rolls Royce, and even had a European gentleman as his chauffeur.

His business success included frequent appearances on national TV talk shows and invitations from the most prestigious organizations worldwide. His audiences are comprised of those wanting to elevate themselves to greater levels.

By the age of forty, Stig earned a multitude of awards for personal excellence and selfless service to humanity. His lifestyle included dining with billionaires and

members of the House of Lords in London. His reach spanned worldwide.

When he turned forty-five, he qualified for the O-1 visa, the hardest in the world to obtain. It is a non-immigrant visa for people with extraordinary abilities of achievements in special fields including business, science, education, athletics, arts, motion picture, and television. Stig was allowed to enter the United States where he later became a legal citizen. His success continued, being blessed to rub shoulders with many of the biggest names in the worlds of business, entertainment, and sports.

Before the great pandemic of 2020, he was being tapped as the talent for high-level gatherings, including speaking at the Mandalay Bay Hotel in Las Vegas at the world's largest real estate educational event. He had achieved the top 1% level as an international speaker and trainer.

* * *

Then his life changed in dramatic ways. Worldwide fear over the pandemic struck, closing down almost all travel, and therefore public speaking—his primary source of income came to a grinding halt. At the same time, the loss of a major long-term relationship broke his heart. The pain of that loss grieved his very soul. He questioned if they ever had a real relationship at all. Nothing in his head made sense anymore. He felt a deep urge to leave the confusion unfolding all around him!

He knew his life "as normal" could not continue. As the world descended into unprecedented chaos, he felt an irresistible calling to go on a solo spiritual vision quest in the desert to seek the voice and will of God.

To fast—to pray—to meditate.

And to remember who he was and to find out where God would take him next. That is the beginning of *Spirit Whispers: Finding Your True Calling in the Stillness.*

Part One
Sojourn

Chapter 1
The Wasteland

When God wants to talk to a man, He often first isolates him.

"God, dear Heavenly Father, Daddy, I come to you with a heart full of love, for you, in my sin and pain, and with a burning desire to take my water to where the thirsty are for your glory. Please kill me now with a lightning bolt, a venomous snake, or with thirst, hunger, heat and/or cold, or please guide me, bless me with my beloved destiny partner and use me for your purposes. Let me please bring glory to you and show the world your goodness."

These are the words I prayed out loud in agony in the Valley of Death during a record-breaking heat wave in the hottest place on Earth, during a sixty-eight-day and night personal vision quest.

"Life happens for you, and through you, not to you
. . ."

The words echoed to me, repeating in my dreams, in my waking hours.

More than a simple proverb, it called to me. Drove me forward.

The words led me from my home in a time of turmoil and unrest deep in my heart. Discord ran through the streets of my hometown, as well, and without a solution or a means to see the troubles gone, I fled.

Out along the old road, a path I had never before taken.

Straight to the edge of the great desert. Bleak and forbidding, many saw it as an unforgiving abyss.

Furnaces have known cooler climes than the scape sweeping out below me.

Sand, cooked rock. A shimmer danced along the surface. Yet a thrill danced along my spine.

This was the adventure I had craved. A challenge worthy of a man I once was, that I longed to be again.

The clear, uncluttered expanse of the unknown whispered to me to let go of all that I held dear and journey into its depths.

Years of order and regimen barked that I should turn around. That I had responsibilities. But those things dulled with the passage of time, like my resolve.

I had been a student, a squire.

A tool, implemented by the system for gain. A soldier, a leader. A teacher.

A man of religion and faith.

An entire life of achievement sprawled like the dunes in the distance along the wake of my journey through this world. Along with a faint sense of impotence and failure to help my people.

When the first of the sick appeared in my homeland, I realized that a hollowness had taken hold and carved out a space within my heart.

Something was missing.

A purpose I once held resolute and without question, now an empty promise. To the vacant, pleading stares of the sick, forced to remain in solitude, I had no response. The healers had their work, and I stood about, eager to assist, but unable to offer any comfort.

So, I turned away, seeking solitude. A break from the noise.

Or perhaps I was a coward.

Either way, I sought a new destination. I hungered for clarity.

And ran from those uncertainties that I could not face.

The years saw to it that my calling was no longer an option. The warrior set down his sword. The captain's men took wives and bore children to a time of peace. And the order that once ruled over my hours left me wandering, lost.

What purpose did I serve in a place where people only need caring hands? What could an old warrior like me offer them?

I admit that melancholy guided my choices too heavily those days leading up to my departure.

And the warm breeze on my face as I rode from the city I once cherished as my home felt like a balm to those woes.

Leaving everything behind set me free from those concerns. Only to find them waiting for me farther down the road. Waiting at the edge of the canyon path before me.

From the distant hills, through the rifts and bluffs of no man's lands, I emerged, caked in dirt. Up the short rise of baked clay, I rose to the rim of the mighty cauldron. There I stood on the edge of the desert, looking out across the desolate landscape, wondering whose voice it was that called me here.

Had I imagined it? No.

Even as I squinted into the afternoon haze, far out over the horizon, it whispered once more, "Life . . ."

Yet before me I saw only death. And the only road left that I had never traveled in these lands. The sparkling wastes, the harshest terrain. Uninhabitable, they say.

Wander, my horse, shifted beneath me, tossing his head at the indecision emanating from his rider. He hated when I dithered and longed to march on. I gave him the choice.

Without a thought to our waning supplies and the

danger ahead, I let Wander do exactly that. Straight into the mouth of the fissure before us. The gateway to the desert that I spent so many nights dreaming of.

The first step was a death unto my old self.

The second, a conviction that I made the right choice in coming here. To be renewed. This was so much easier said and imagined than done.

Certainly, even more so when a great wind rose to meet us, blasting my face and exposed arms with grit and dust, coiling up around my faithful mount's hooves and whipping viciously into our eyes. Every violent gust carried with it the doleful moan of suffering, the singed scent of arid, burnt sand.

But I have never been one to back down from a challenge. Nor have I ever learned easily the lessons the universe so generously offers.

The third strike of hoof drew me up short, tugging on the reins as a calamity of clattering wood echoed behind me, startling Wander and nearly unseating me. Settling him, I turned back to see the source of the sudden noise.

"Heading into the wastes, traveler?" a deep voice called from below, from the folds of fabric wrapped against the wind. Despite the flowing coils of cloth, he sat tall on the bench of his weather-worn wagon, broad-shouldered, yet slouched with the posture of one accustomed to the road.

The ox pulling the thing had seen better days but seemed hardly concerned with Wander or my presence.

Would that I might find that sort of peace, in simple tasks and chewing cud.

"The thought had crossed my mind to cross these lands," I replied, trotting down the slope to meet the stranger.

"Hmm," he hummed, and I heard his smile as bright eyes met mine. Lines around those vibrant eyes put mine to shame, belying the great many years this still robust fellow had on me. "You should turn back. That way lies danger. Pain. Death. And worse."

Though his voice remained pleasant, something in his warning rang hard against my chest. This was a man knowledgeable in such things.

"What could be worse than such as those?"

This time his grin tugged down the swath of his headdress, showing a prominent beard, rife with gray. "Fear. Isolation. Truth."

"Fear chases behind me as well. It chases us all."

"So do you run from it or seek it out?" He challenged.

"The same could be said of truth," I remarked, feeling the pull of a smile at my own lips.

"Out there you face them both. It is no easy task."

"I am prepared for whatever might lie ahead."

"Hmm. So you say. What is it you hope to find?" the man asked.

"The voice of the desert. It called to me."

"Many have heard her cry. But there is nothing out there, young Stig." How did this man know my name?

The way he spoke, it sang like a title over me, though I was far from young.

"I beg to differ. You said it yourself, there is Truth. I would find him anew."

"Ah, I see. Then I must see you provisioned well." He gestured to his cart, and the wares packed under the tarp. "For there is little supply to be found out there, save what you take with you."

"I thank you, Peddler."

We exchanged a few more quips about the weather and the heat as I stocked up on rations, water, and other items he insisted I would need. Handing him payment, he took the coins hesitantly, gazing past me into the wasteland.

"Take care, Stig."

"Do not worry about me, old man. I am versed in survival."

"That is only one of the trials you will face. Take care of your mind and your spirit. The desert cares little for your body. She will drink your sorrow. Draw out your anguish."

"She will try."

Mounting Wander, I wrapped my face, mimicking his motions as he again took his place on his bench. Our eyes met once more, and I nodded, rounding back toward the bitter road ahead.

"Once you enter, there is no turning back, Stig."

A strange thing to say, I thought. But it did not give me pause.

"Oh, and don't forget to drink water, even when you are not thirsty," he shouted over his shoulder.

"And where does one find water in the desert, Peddler?" I asked, taking a deep breath.

"Just over the next hill," he hollered, popping the reins and setting a clattering pace down the road.

A chuckle shook my shoulders as I trotted Wander back to the edge of the path. I glanced back just once over my shoulder as we set off.

And the old man was gone.

Stig's Journal, Day 1

This is the Time I am given

I have but one life. I will live it—fully.

The desert is a desolation, but for me, it will be a training ground. I take with me a deep and passionate need to be whole once more. To be better. Stronger.

May compassion be a guiding force for me on my journey.

May love find a hold in my heart again. For myself. For the offerings of the world and the universe. This time is mine, to spend in my own company. To learn who I really am.

I will not fall to fear. I will not stumble.

I will block out my time, a routine of progress, in milestones and goals. This journal will stand as a testament to my mission

Prayer

Speak to me, and I will listen. Gifts have been given to all of us. Vitality. Talents. Guide me toward mercy and forgiveness. May I become a better person.

Am I open to seeing the gifts I have been given?

Take stock in the state of my being:

Am I who I want to be?

Am I healthy?

What is the state of my mind as I enter this challenge?

Chapter 2

The Horse, the Coyote, and the Scorpion

"Survival in the desert starts with knowing the greatest threats: Dress appropriately. Wear lightweight, light-colored clothing to reflect the sun's heat and protect yourself from sunburn. Cover exposed skin. Bundle up at night." Peddler's parting advice stayed with me.

"Know your surroundings. Find high ground when you can. A signal mirror can save your life if you are lost. Breathe through your nose. Stay calm. It is easy to panic in a survival situation. Focus on your breathing, and ask yourself, what is my best next action to take now? Finally, Conserve energy. Food and water must last as long as possible."

"Anything else?" I asked.

"Yes. Always carry a good knife."

* * *

"Wander, I think the Peddler was being literal," I muttered, already parched, my mouth longing for moisture.

Looking back up the narrow and treacherous cliff-side, I knew without any doubt that there was no going back up that incline. Most of the way down had been a negotiation for our lives.

My heart still pounding, I led my horse from the looming canyon wall and turned toward the vast plateau of dunes rolling away into the distance.

An hour later, I knew we needed to find shelter to wait out the hottest stretch of the day.

This was a lesson taught to any survivalist early on, to travel early in the morning or into the evening, to sleep out the heat of the day.

But I could hardly navigate the cliffside in the dark. So, we trudged on for almost an hour before I spotted an outcropping of stones where I could pin my tarp against the onslaught of the sun. It was under that temporary and insufficient shelter that I met Loneliness for the first time. She came to me rather abruptly, offering me a dour sort of companionship that I was not accustomed to. I had not experienced such a feeling in quite some time.

After the initial pang of her presence, a dull ache in my heart, I welcomed her.

Was this not precisely why I came to this land, to find solitude?

Yet I suppose I did not fully understand what it meant to be truly alone until she joined me and whispered longing and forlorn remembrances of my home into my ear. The comforts of my rooms. My books. Tea and coffee and unlimited water.

Having so long lived in the company of others, I struggled to reconcile this intense solitude.

Most of my life had been spent in fellowship, companionship: my siblings as a child, my friends throughout my schooling, my fellow soldiers in arms, and then the own men of my company under me, and later, my students, the congregation of my church . . . Many of them remained back home, though the years had grown long between us.

Some had mocked my sojourn. Others disapproved. Many of them condemned me outright for this venture. Their harsh words still ringing in my ears.

And it was those voices that accompanied Loneliness, filling my lean-to with discontent, doubt.

She stayed with me those first few days.

Through the waking hours, often walking beside my mount, dragging my feet through loose sand. And throughout the rest of the day, reminding me in my fitful dreams of expectations and the impatience to make my discovery so that I might return with great inspiration.

Such thoughts haunted and consumed me before long. As one does, I dwelled on each thought that came to mind with nothing else to distract me. Could such endless pondering drive a man to madness in this solitary state? I had ignored the risks; whether an act of bravery or a death wish would eventually be revealed.

I became a part of the sandscapes and bleak rock around me during those times of deep thought. Just like those silent landmarks, I sat still in the fires of the day, waiting for the face of the sun to wane in its passage before continuing on, eager to find some task to put myself to.

With only my horse for company, I soon became cross. Thirsty. Hungry.

Those long hours of waiting became a source of frustration. Which inevitably led me to make a foolish choice. Shortly after setting my tarp, one of the ties came loose. In anger I tore the whole thing down, stuffing it into my saddlebag.

Riding in the blistering glare, I guided my mount onward, determined to find some better cover or a source of reprieve from the misery of sweat. For an hour I stomped along, urging my ride behind me by the reins despite his protests to stop and conserve our energy.

Funny how man trivializes the wisdom of instinct, the natural inclination of the beasts. And even more than wisdom, the simple logical sense to know better.

Ah, but animals are proud too, at times, as I would discover soon enough.

My senses heightened as I stomped through the silence, only my crunching boots breaking the stillness. My sight smothered in blinding white and the shade of my head wrap, I could only listen for telltale signs of danger. So too, did my nose compensate for the utter dryness in my mouth and throat, scenting my own sweat prominently and the lather on Wander's flanks.

It was in this heightened state that I clearly smelled a faint hint of moisture on the air.

Yet as we kept walking, I found not a hint of water. "Over the next hill, indeed," I snapped, hunkering down to make camp.

As the day drew to a close and exhaustion took me, I laughed, somewhat bitterly. For I had not in fact found a single hill as of yet.

The chill of the desert night crept in, and I wrapped my blanket tightly around me, falling into a restless sleep. In the dead of night, I woke, Wander nickering softly in the cold.

My ears perked up, noting the sounds around me. A persistent scuttling and scurrying that put me on edge.

I was not alone.

The desert night was filled with scores of creatures creeping in the dark, slithering, skittering about in the dark. And further away, yips and howls traversed the landscape, teasing my imagination with images of hunting rabbits, rushing over the dunes to catch a meal. Or hurrying into a den in the nick of time, safely out of reach. Sitting up, I rubbed my arms. A fire sounded more than appealing.

Fortunately, I had the perfect fuel at hand and soon felt the warm glow of a pungent dung fire. It barely emanated light, but the heat rolled off toward me, forming a circle of safety from the frigid air.

For an hour I sat, staring into the embers, lost in memories. Letting my mind drift.

Until early in the morning I noticed that Wander stood completely still. His ears pressed to his head.

Glancing across the remains of my fire, through the wafting smoke, I caught the gleam of starlight in two glistening eyes. As my sight adjusted to the surprisingly illuminating starlight drifting from above, I made out the distinct shape of a coyote, jet black against the deep blue gray of the sand.

He looked right at me; his head tilted to one side. And there we sat for some time; our eyes locked in the uncertainty of one another. Until he glanced down, once. Carefully, slowly, I ignited a bit more dried horse dung, bringing back the warmth of the embers. Then I laid down, never taking my eyes off my new companion. As I cradled my head once more on my saddlebag, the coyote mimicked my movement, laying down and crossing his paws. His body curled in an arc to match the shape of our ring of luxurious heat, and he closed his eyes.

Just like that, loneliness had no business in my camp, and I knew true rest. As if the spirit of the coyote guarded my dreams against any foul presence.

So, the legends say.

I rose just before sunrise, finding my guardian long gone, but it would not be the last that I saw of him. Another morning of walking, an afternoon spent huddled against an old stone well, long dry, and evening found me once more sitting in the dark.

He again appeared, this time much more boldly. And

again, he left before the sun, nodding once to me this time as if to finalize our agreement.

Would that I had asked him where to find water. For the next day, my canteen ran dry.

"Life . . ." the voice of the desert whispered, and I sat up, listening with my entire being, basking in the last gust of chill night air.

She said nothing else, but I followed the path of that wind.

We walked, Wander staggering along behind me through the morning.

Long before the sun reached its zenith, I set my tarp, rolled up beneath it and fell sound asleep. Wander slumped to his belly, then onto his side. He was fading. Driven too far for too long.

"Wake up, Stig," a soft voice hissed, and I bolted upright, pain lancing my body.

And with it, a deep, horrific thirst. A fever. Immediately I reached for any sort of weapon, knowing that my enclosure had been invaded. That I had been stung by the desert.

Scrambling to my haunches, I put my back to the tarp, shaking out my blanket, prepared to strike. I raised my tack hammer, pausing at the sight of the black carapace. The stinger. The pincers.

She's huge. Which means her sting is likely not fatal. Just very painful.

And like a memory returning, or a dream manifesting

behind my eyes, I hear a conversation from deep in the night. The coyote sits across from me, keenly focused eyes watching me as I sleep.

"Each night you come. Is it to watch over me? Or do you wait, to make of me a meal, brother?" I asked, my voice drenched in sleep still.

Coyote sighed, tilting his head as he did, a mocking smile passing over his gleaming teeth.

"You are foolish to venture into such a place where you do not belong, human." Coyote's tongue lolled in the dim light of the fire. "But you shared your warmth. So, I guard your sleep."

"And who watches over me in the day when I hide from the sun?"

"The heat itself deters threats. But beware. Such shelter attracts unwanted guests," he reminded me.

"The only threat I face now is a lack of water." I wipe dust from my eye.

"Then perhaps such unwanted guests might be of use. In more ways than one…"

In an instant, the vision is gone.

The scorpion didn't waste time in my hesitation, bolting for an opening in the fabric.

And I do not lose the opportunity to give chase, for even the critters of the desert need water.

Outside the tent, the day is still an inferno, as though the very surface of the sun had touched the earth, but my focus is razor sharp on the black glint of shell rushing

away. So engrossed was I in chasing the creature down, I barely noticed the change in the incline of the land, the sand sloping up, up, up and over.

On the far side of the hill, I spotted the scorpion's destination, and a wild grin spread over my face. Without a second thought, I scrambled down the slope, tumbling once before I reached the patch of moist dirt on my knees, digging in with a ferocity driven by desperation and just a hint of madness from the several stings along my back and leg.

A foot down, muddy water leeched to the surface. Glorious.

Movement caught my eye as I snatched my waterskin, aiming to fill it quickly, to return to Wander before filling the rest of our supply. The scorpion skittered down into the depression I dug, indifferent to my presence.

Anger rose at the audacity of the creature, uncaring of the pain it caused me.

But a thought occurred to me then, as I noted the way the scorpion ignored me. Her purpose was singular. To drink. To eat. To survive.

With a swift flick of my wrist, I snatched the scorpion, flipping her onto a stone and driving my hammer down, once, twice. As I did, I prayed to the desert, asking for the means I needed to survive.

"If you are to be a pain to me, then I ask that you also be a weapon!" I strike again, honing with each blow, this creature designed to thrive in this wasteland, into a tool. A weapon.

A knife. Jet black and sharp as the tip of the scorpion's tail.

Raising the crude dagger, I admired my handiwork with wide eyes, tucking it into my belt.

Then I drank deep of the small pool, slaking my intense thirst. Finished, I stumbled back to Wander and my gear, knowing before I arrived that he was no more. For he had been stung more than I, and by the deadly variety of scorpions, small and white.

"Old friend, I am sorry," I sang, patting his flank gently. A tear for his passing formed in my eye. "Thank you for your spirit. For your loyalty and love. And for your sacrifice."

Then I began doing what needed doing.

Once my pack was full of as much water and meat as I could carry, I set out again in the deep red of dusk, needing to be as far from that place as I could get. Sleep would not come to me that night, nor my guardian.

Though I saw him from afar, keeping pace in his nightly hunt.

Stig's Journal, Day 5

I create my purpose, in my time.

I am in the middle of nowhere, with nothing. Now truly alone.

The air here sears my lungs.

The cold at night seeks to freeze me solid.

The anvil lies beneath me, this cracked ground. The hammer bears down on me from above, glowing with the heat of the forge-fire.

Do I have what it takes to see this journey through?

Am I to be formed into something greater, or obliterated and cast aside?

Time hones us in different ways; will we become a tool for good? A weapon for evil?

The hero's journey reveals the answer. It begins and ends with purpose; a lesson taught through trial and time. Somewhere in the middle, choices must be made that forge a person into greatness. Or shatter them.

Prayer

What is beyond the horizon? Do I see what lies ahead of me, always looking far away toward the future?

I ask to be present in my life. In my time.

Who am I now? Who do I want to be? I only become that person if I begin in this moment.

Why am I here? Not a question of things thrust upon me, but a recognition of my decisions that led to this place.

Chapter 3

The Crow and the Peddler

A great man once said, "Ask of God, of your-self, and of others."

Asking of the Source comes naturally in times of need, yet we should do so at all times. Asking of yourself is born in discipline and survival. Asking of others requires taming our pride. All three are crucial to our success.

Midday marked two weeks in the desert.

Strange how long such a span can feel. How rapidly it can slip by.

I was much farther along, yet not one step closer to my destination. For when you have nowhere in partic-ular to go, everywhere is exactly where you are meant to be. Or perhaps those are just the musings of a man driven mad by solitude and intolerable heat.

The days passed, each lasting far longer than its hours. I grew ever more exhausted, my mind sharing the travail of my body.

Carrying the extra weight of cured meat and water added to my efforts, but I could hardly go on without the sustenance to maintain me. Still, it was a relief and an ironic blessing as my bag got lighter.

Of course, that inevitably meant I would run out of food all too soon. But the desert provides. Or perhaps it's the whispers of the spirit, fate or God. Either way, I had survived, and I knew I would continue to do so.

"Where must I go, brother?" I asked my quiet companion sitting by the fire again one night.

He raised his ears, tuning into the sounds of the desert, then slowly blinked his eyes, always loath to give me counsel.

"Onward." Coyote's message was clear and simple.

Of course, his purpose was not to lead me to my destination. Only to guard me as I rested. And to be my teacher in the small ways of the desert.

"If you cannot be my eyes, I surely must find a guide, then."

"As you will, little brother. My nose is my guide. My ears are my warning of danger. Last are my eyes to spot my meals." His eyes glistened in the moonlight.

"Alas, but my senses are not as acute as yours, brother." I shook my head.

"Clearly. Humans seem to only use their ears to listen to themselves talk."

"That and to weather rude comments from coyotes." I grinned.

Sitting alone in the sliver of meager shade from a dead and withered tree the next day, I pondered which way I might go. Some semblances of a road appeared to pass beside this post, yet in either direction it faded within a mile, swallowed up by the endless sea of sand. The desert does not long suffer the traces of man on her surface. So, I sat, my back to the petrified trunk.

What the shade did not cover, my robes and wrap did, keeping me from scorching in the sun. Even so, my skin stung in places from being so long outdoors. Still better than blisters. Such an infection would surely lead to my demise. Just as impatience had led to my early mistakes. I spent long hours absorbed in thought, lost deep within myself staring into the sprawling wastes during the peak hours. I longed for night at those times, when we might confer again, Coyote and me. After sharing my meat with him, he had shared in turn the spoils of his hunts, buying me a few more meals.

More than that, I simply enjoyed his company. His lessons and his tales.

The safety of his presence. The absence of dark dreams.

Unlike when I slept during the day. Then, the stresses of my old life manifested. Memories and failures. They seemed to grow heavier in the light, weighing me down until darkness fell again.

Even more so when my spirits drifted into the shadowy recesses of my mind. The threat of never re-emerging from that dark internal place hung over me ominously.

A cloud seemed to settle overhead, the shadow of the tree expanding into an odd shape on the ground at my feet. My breath hitched in my chest, tremors of apprehension climbing up my spine.

"Heavy, too heavy," a voice croaked above me.

The creature cocked its head as I turned, looking down with one onyx eye, fluffing out black feathers. His presence shook me from my meditations, something ringing familiarly in the back of my mind.

A crow. Another omen.

For crows are long of memory, deep of sight. Helpful, but mischievous. And they're always ready to bargain.

"Too heavy for you? I suppose I am. Would that I might ride your wing above the ground, good bird. That I might see where I need to go."

"Too heavy indeed. Just like your purse. It weighs you down, so full. So useless."

"True. You see much. But I do not believe that I have anything in this purse of worth to your honorable self that I might offer in exchange for the privilege of your guidance."

"Empty of belly you are, but not of wit. It seems you see just fine, if believing comes from sight. Flattery, however, you have in spades."

"Then consider me a wealthy man, Crow. But courtesy should always be offered generously, and free of charge." I smirked.

At this, he cackled, cawing out over the plain and dancing back and forth from foot to foot. "This game, a

trade could be, of words and knowledge you have for me."

"Hardly a fair trade for saving my life, simple words." I argued.

"Ah, but words hold value when spun into tales and verse."

"Only such value as the listener applies," I retorted.

"A test then. You tell me one morsel, and I will take wing. What I bring in return will be of equal value to that thing," Crow bargained, raising his wings importantly.

My eyes narrowed at the beast, a smile cracking my lip, accepting his offer. Or was it rather a challenge?

He might try to deceive me. Mislead me even. But with nothing to lose, I might at least get a good laugh out of a trickster's prank before I perished. With a nod, I rose to face him.

"Here then, a payment. Consider this: I left my home, seeking answers to questions I do not know how to vocalize. Choosing to become lost, I am now vexed by the very fact that I do not know which way to go. Have I then found exactly what I sought when I entered the desert?"

"A loop! A circle! Much to digest!" he sang, shaking out his plumage.

With a somewhat irritated clack of his beak he took flight, soaring up away from me. In moments he was out of sight, swooping down behind the dunes to my left.

An hour passed. I drifted into a light sleep.

When I stirred occasionally from my slumber, I convinced myself that the crow must have been a dream. That or he moved on, considering my riddle nonsense, which it was.

Until the flap of wings startled me from my repose, followed by the familiar clatter of wagon wheels on the hard packed dirt. As if out of thin air, the Peddler appeared in the distance, around a bend in the road I swear had not been there earlier. The sight of him shocked me so, that I nearly scrambled for cover.

At the same time, my heart leapt at the idea of company and the racing thoughts of what he might offer me from his stock. Surely, he would have food. Water.

The wagon shuddered to a halt in front of me, the strange man glancing down at me. How pitiful I must have looked. Yet he did not sneer, nor flinch at the sight of me.

"Well then," he mused, nodding once. "Not as well as I would like."

"Precisely. You think it chance that brings our paths together once more?"

With a flick of his wrist, he guided the ox off the road a bit, waving for me to follow. As I stood, I could see him there, the crow perched on the back of the wagon as though he owned it.

"This is your trade then, for my words?"

"A worthy payment for something so confounding as your journey," Crow cackled, flapping across the

distance to land on my outstretched arm. "You presented me with a paradox. So, I brought you a cart, and an ox!" With that, and a nip at my sleeve, he soared away.

By the time I stood at the Peddler's wagon, the man had set a canvas and stones for a fire. A small yet pristine camp welcomed me as the sun began to arch toward the horizon, the sun catching on a neat circle of stones tucked in a crevasse of sandstone.

A well . . . it could not be . . . but it was.

"Sit. Eat. Drink. Be well," he invited me, smiling. A beautiful blanket, awash in bright colors, awaited me under the cover of his canopy, but I frowned down at my filthy state.

"I am content to sit out here," I offered.

"Are we to battle for who is most courteous?"

"I would not impose on a stranger."

"Consider yourself a customer, then. And my guest. If not that, then simply adhere to water etiquette. Friend, foe, predator and prey all drink in peace at the watering hole."

His words dismissed my misgivings. Washing my hands and face in the basin, I closed my eyes, savoring the sensation. I had not been so refreshed in what felt like a lifetime.

Soon, we lay back in the cool of the tent, sharing the luxury of a cooked meal.

"I fear I am lost, Peddler."

"Being lost is one thing. Being lost and afraid, another."

"I am not afraid of hardship." I straightened my back.

"Certainly not. You came this far already."

"Perhaps that is the sum total of my journey. To live out my days here." I shook my head.

"Perhaps. I do not think so. Either way, you must cross the desert. There is no going back."

Nothing he said came as news to me. Yet something in his words rang profoundly true in my heart. That I must keep moving above all else. Because to stagnate would be to lose all hope. To lose the small purpose I had of at least putting one foot in front of the other would surely defeat me. More than thirst or hunger.

Giving up would destroy my spirit.

"Many days ago, I asked you what you hoped to find. What have you found, thus far?" he asked.

"I first found Loneliness. Faced her and made peace with her. I have learned many lessons in patience since then. I have also been foolish. I have taken risks. I have failed many times."

"You have made friends, too. Follow the teachings of your companions." The Peddler nodded as though he knew of my journey.

"I am learning wisdom. Slowly."

"Then it is wisdom earned," Peddler assured me.

To that, all I could do was nod. Looking around at the bounty and comfort offered to me by my host, emotion swept over me, overwhelming me. Emotions I'd forgotten I even had.

"I wonder, Peddler, are you, the crow, and the coyote angels sent to protect me, to guide me?"

"In a way. We are all angels on this Earth, Stig. Every one of us has the capacity to do great good. To bless others. To serve one another, is to resemble the angels in their glory."

His words sang to me as my eyes grew heavy. Laying my head down, I watched the shadow of Coyote in the distance, climbing a dune. Calling out into the night under a crescent moon.

He called to me. To drive the darkness of shadows from our camp. When I woke, many hours later, the Peddler was gone. Only his canopy remained above me. And perched on the corner post, a familiar creature, smiling down on me.

"Rise, Stig. There is much to see," Crow cawed. With renewed energy, I broke camp, setting off as my guide soared above me. Leading me toward hope and purpose.

Stig's Journal, Day 15

Dictating my Energy

At times I feel deeply alone and scared. Wondering if the universe, God, the spirits of the desert will ever answer my pleas, my prayers. Was my journey in vain?

I am nothing, I have nothing. Living here in the wastes like a homeless wretch. A desert rat. I feel like a rag, wrung out. Tossed aside.

Will I die here alone in these badlands?

It is up to Him, to fate. The will of the infinite.

Prayer

Cleanse my thoughts of venom.

*Purge my anger and my self-doubt. Bolster my will
and my discipline.*

My energies are wasted resisting the temptations of the flesh.

*Constantly worrying about the darkness inside me, the
shadows roiling in my soul.*

I long for companionship.

May I give thanks when it arrives, in any form.

*Ground me in the land, let my bare feet feel the earth
and its stability.*

*Charge me from the air, let my breath fill me with light.
Sustain me*

Chapter 4

The Shadow

*U*nderstanding our place in the cycle is everything.

The Universe is benevolent and wants the best for all of us.

Suffering is good; it brings us into a deeper, more sincere conversation and relationship with the Source. With Life.

It is a gift.

Embrace it with joy. Learn and grow.

But remember, too much suffering can break you down. Our deepest wounds can destroy us. Or they can become our greatest blessing, and our message to help others. Our greatest struggles can become our life's work.

Two nights later, the road Crow led me along disappeared underfoot without warning, and I found myself standing at the base of a twisting canyon. Without backtracking, there was no way around.

What food I had left from my trade with the Peddler was soon to spoil, and I knew I would share the last of it with my companions that very day.

Wearily, I debated stopping for the night or pressing on. I had water for another day, maybe more.

"Is this a challenge, Crow?"

"Only if you cannot sprout wings and fly with me across," he called down.

"Will you not guide me through this maze, then?"

"There is but one way through. But it is not a labyrinth of rock, but of the mind. My kind do not trespass below. We do not care for such confinement."

"I admit that I am not fond of it myself. But if there is no other way . . ." I answered.

With no other option, I headed into the thin mouth of the canyon.

The one saving grace was that it blocked the sun, keeping its aggression from my back, although in the past several days I had taken to traveling more during the evening.

In open spaces that was all well, but I knew the dangers of traversing the canyon in the dark. Not only would I be completely blind, but I would also no doubt tread upon a serpent or stumble through a deadly spider's web without light. With a deep breath and a tight grip on my discomfort, I pushed forward.

Many hours went by, the strange nature of the walls warping every sound. After so many days out in the expanses of the dunes, this place indeed felt oppressively tight.

So much so, that I began to imagine that I was being followed. That I was pursued.

When that sensation passed, the strain of solitude impinged on my mind, pressing in even closer than the granite on all sides. I began to believe that I would never leave this dreadful place, that it was in fact an impassable maze, and that I had already taken a wrong turn. That I circled and circled for hours, days.

Even though it does appear to only go in one direction.

Soon the shadows of night start to come. They always come sooner in the darkening canyon until I can barely see in front of me, finding the nook, a small enclosure. Without any suitable dung for a fire, I give in, desperate for warmth.

Gathering old wood, twigs and roots, I lit a fire, smoking terribly and casting long shadows astride the canyon walls.

Still, it settled some unease within me, to have light and warmth.

I curse my foolish decision not to wait another day, to start out earlier. And I curse my hesitant pace for not clearing this place before nightfall or finding a better place to camp. The nook is defensible, yes, but it feels even more confining as the deep dark of the night draws its curtains over the land.

No hint of moonlight reached me.

No glow of the stars. I was blinded to them all by the glare of my fire.

A fitting grave, where no one would ever find me.

I almost laughed at my plight, yet another foolish situation befalling me on my quest. It seemed that each time I attempted to avoid catastrophe, I tumbled headlong into its path.

Eventually, exhaustion bested me, and I drifted.

For a time, I drifted in and out of anxious memories, dreams. The cold rock behind my back added to the discomfort. Yet I never quite woke. As I never quite slept. My heightened senses registered movement in the dark. Sounds in the night.

But I had checked my dwelling carefully.

There were no signs of life in the canyon. I knew it to be a place of absence, one of the dead places.

Which is why Crow and Coyote would not join me here. They knew better.

"There are depths in the desert. Places the living must not wander," Coyote had warned me one evening.

"These places, they are dangerous?"

"Yes. Deadly." Coyote cautioned. "But not for the predators or toxic plants that reside there."

"You mean poison? Like leaking miasma from the soil?"

"In a few cases, yes," he said.

"And the others?" I asked.

"The others are soulless. Bright and dark at the same time. Devoid of life."

I knew at once this was such a place. The faint scent I had not been able to place since entering lingered in my nostrils. Sulfur. Other toxic scents. The very rock seemed designed to prevent life from taking hold. Only death and decay could thrive here.

Scholars in my country had studied such chemicals, finding them inimical to all living things. This is why I found not a serpent, not a single insect in my camp.

I opened my eyes, staring up into the vault of the sky, the faint glow of my fire dimming in the early hours. Quiet hung heavily over the land. A dark presence loomed nearer.

Sitting up, I gazed across the dwindling remains of my fire.

The shadowy figure sat very still. Watching me. He was tall. Broad. Something in the shift of his shoulders, the tilt of his head, reminded me of someone I knew long ago. And with those memories, sorrow. Doubt. Anguish. He rose as I did, pacing the other side of the fire, across the opening to the enclosure. Blocking my path. Where he stood was the purest darkness, the deepest shadow. For he was one with that void. He was one with the dead earth surrounding me.

"Finally," he whispered, singing to me in a voice that drew me in, begging me to listen. "You are alone. You have come to me to absolve your sins."

"No . . ." I protested, my hands shaking.

A most primal fear took hold in my chest, that the embers of my fire would extinguish, that the light would go out. The very stars abandoned me there, and I would surely be dragged down into the depths if the light went out.

I would be eaten alive, swallowed by terror. No. I will not, I thought.

I rose, clenching my fists, glaring at my opponent. My tormentor. He only mimicked my movements, matching my steps around the fire, keeping pace as I circled. His posture was everything mine was not. Domineering, his sneer a vicious contrast to my terrified grimace.

But his eyes watched me warily, as I watched him. Shadow stalked me, as I tried and failed to remain calm. To put on a show of bravery. All in vain.

It is as if he knew my every weakness.

"Will you run screaming, coward?" he chuckled, mocking my glances toward the exit.

"No. I have never run from anything."

"Right. Because you are so proud. So much so that you cannot ever let anyone see you falter."

"Many have. I have never hidden my failures."

"Another attempt to be a so-called 'great man.' To own every mistake. To apologize quickly. They don't see what lies behind the platitudes. The mask that you wear to hide your hypocrisy," his voice full of judgment.

"I wear no mask, Shadow."

"No, not here. Yet here you are. Far from home. Far from anyone who would judge you. A shell of yourself. Free from responsibility."

"I came here to . . ."

"Hide," he finishes.

I felt a rush of shame, a flood of blood reaching my cheeks.

He was not entirely wrong. Still, anger rose, denial. "Won't you sit with me, Shadow?" My righteous anger lent me strength, overcoming the initial shock of his intrusion. "We can talk. Just let us do so calmly. As friends, even."

"You do not truly welcome me. But I will sit."

He mirrored me again and we faced one another, the glow of the fire accenting the rocks, the sand. But not his face. It remained utterly dark. Empty, save for his contemptuous smile.

"I would offer you food or water, but I have none. They have all been used up, and if I do not find any tomorrow, well, I fear I may join you in the darkness forever." My bluff hides behind a chuckle, as hollow as his eyes.

"There you are. The politician. The speaker. If you make the failure your own, contextualize it with humor, perhaps the fault will not belong to you."

"Humor certainly helps lighten the mood," I responded.

"A weapon, then. Or a tool?" he challenged.

"Neither. Humor is a boon. A gift." I defended.

"A stopgap. A temporary shield. Against worry. Against fear. But they remain on the other side of the barrier. Waiting for you." His words bore deeply.

"Yes. And I face them when I am ready. With the weapons of love and compassion."

"The weapons you hold are dull and brittle, Stig!" he shouted into my heart, without raising his voice.

"Nonetheless, I hold to them," I whispered, my resolve crumbling under his verbal assault.

"That is what brought you to the desert in the first place, was it not? The desire to obliterate fear? To destroy worry. By abandoning the very source of that woe? Sounds like running away to me."

A part of me wanted to rail against what he was saying, to deny his claims. But an ache started deep in my chest, a sorrow for those I left behind. My family, my uncle, my mother. And further back, echoing over the years in disappointment. My grandparents, long dead. My father, more recently.

Loneliness joined us then, silent and leeching.

She drew on my will more than she ever had, wearing me down. Darkening the flames of my campfire. Shadow seemed to drink in even more depth, growing more menacing across from me.

"Pathetic. You sit out here alone, and for what? Why did you come to this place? Are you but waiting

to die?" Shadow growled, his snide demeanor falling to aggression.

"This is my penance. My crucible," I gasped.

With a dismissive shrug, Shadow opened his hands in sympathy, a hopeless gesture. "You thought yourself bold. Brave."

"I did not . . . I was simply . . ." I stuttered.

"A coward," he finishes, his grin returning in malicious glee.

The sting of his words bites deep, eating into me, as bitter as the chill wind that cut through the canyon in that moment.

"I do not . . . I do not wish to play host to you any longer!" I cried. "Nor house these bleak thoughts!"

"You would have better luck cutting off your own hand, Stig."

Bile seeped into me from his mouth. "These are the truths of your soul, ingrained in your bones. You are a sinner. A sycophant. A slave to your vices!" Shadow said, rising to his feet in fluid motion, circling the flames and looming beside me. There he crouched low, whispering in my ear.

I could not move, frozen and chilled to the bone.

"Listen closely, my friend, my child, my brother: giving up is not a sin. It is simply natural. Now go to sleep. Rest your eyes. I shall even lend you my coat to keep you warm."

His hands wrapped around my shoulders, dragging the heavy drape of his darkness across me. "All you need to do is wrap yourself in it and drift off."

At the edges of my vision the pitch-black cloak writhed, reaching for me. And despite my revulsion at the sight of such a detestable thing, it calls to me, as a long-lost memory from my past. Familiar warmth of the way things used to be; of the way I used to be.

A younger man, an angry man, making poor choices, driving those around me away, running away to join the army. Fleeing my responsibilities. Training and shutting off the parts of me that I did not want to see. Ignoring the scars I gave to others and the ones I placed on myself. Willfully blind to my failures and transgressions.

The old ways, the despair and anger enveloped me as Shadow pushed me down, urging me to rest. Covering me in his cloak.

Something stirred in my heart, a distant voice, begging me to stop him. Telling me that the fears and doubts of my past that reside in this dark place would drag me down. Warning that if I dove into those waters, I would never surface.

The darkness began to swallow me whole.

Stig's Journal, Day 27

Mindfulness and doubt.

This path is so difficult. Mentally, nearly unbearable at times.

The desert has proven more challenging than anything I have ever encountered, beyond what I could have anticipated. Yet each day I find a sight truly unimaginable in the vast expanse. Colors I have never seen. Distance and scale unfathomable.

So, the struggle is beautiful.

Yet I have not heard the voice again, the one that called me here.

Will I ever hear it again?

Prayer

Brother, why did I come here?

What do I seek to discover this day?

*Let me take stock of my body, my mind. Take note of my
ailment and my health. What hurts?*

*What pains can be alleviated? What do I need to thrive, to
recharge and be whole again?*

*The wellness I desire, the prosperity is just out of reach. May
I grasp them.*

Take hold of them and make them mine.

Heal my life.

*I must ask, what is holding me from my freedom? And
who, or what could I hurt by seeking that goal? Eat. Sleep.
Hydrate. Exercise. These are the ways to maintain the body.*

Meditate. Breathe. Process.

These are the ways to maintain the mind.

Chapter 5

The Hunter and the Scout

*O*ur greatest failure is to rely only on our own knowledge and opinions.

Worse, we only offer prayers when things get difficult.

The divine is all around us. But we are blind. We are stubborn.

A great upheaval is necessary to break our concentration on ourselves. To make us look around at the world. And when we do, we rarely see what is offered to us. The whole world is a teacher. Each experience a lesson.

Divine, self, and the souls of others. These are the opportunities for knowing what we have all around us. A sharp yelp split the silence of the night as my eyes began to drift closed, startling me awake.

Right before a flicker of movement rushed through the entrance to my camp, scattering the ashes from the fire, spraying embers into Shadow's face. He recoiled with a shriek.

Instantly, the camp was much darker, but the stark contrast of shadows was gone with the light of the fire snubbed out. And with it, the vacuum of dread pulling me under, evaporated.

Before the wrath of my rescuer, Shadow fled, a low snarl echoing after him through the canyon.

The silent Hunter waited by the gap in the rock, listening closely, before sighing and turning back toward me. I sat still as he approached, bending down and drawing out his knife. With a quick slash, he tattered Shadow's cloak into ribbons and the inky black melted into the ground. In the wake of that weight lifting off of me, I sat up, gasping in relief.

"Thank you, stranger," I stammered, wrapping my arms about myself for warmth.

Yet he said nothing, rising and moving away from me. As he did, I watched him shift, down to all fours and I knew him for my guardian, Coyote. In my darkest hour, he came to save me. Even in this horrid place.

"Brother," I began, unsure of how to apologize, or how to explain.

"Sleep, now," he commanded, shaking his head once as he sat near me, keeping watch. "Tomorrow we must be gone from here."

Suddenly, my head swam with the exhaustion of a day's travel, my chin dropping to my chest. Without protest, I sagged to my side, wrapping myself in my bedroll.

I fell into a deep sleep in seconds. All through the night, Coyote stood guard.

"Stig." His only word drew me back to consciousness some hours later.

Gathering my things, I followed quickly, still shaking the vestiges of my ordeal and too little sleep from my aching limbs. Even so, with hurried purpose and a desperate desire to be free of this place, I picked up my pace.

"I should never have come here."

"There was no option. At times we must pass through fire to reach our destinations," Coyote said softly. "You must always grow in knowledge to be ever prepared to succeed when such a challenge arrives."

After a lifetime of lessons and study, I often felt in those days that I had little left to learn. Following in the pattering steps of my companion, Humility joined us that day.

Not only in the signs that Coyote pointed out.

Warnings of danger and the desert's inimitable way of giving directions to its inhabitants lay at every turn if one knew what to look for. And show me he did.

More than this, however, Humility glanced back at me frequently, nodding as I doggedly kept up with my guide. Coyote set a brutal pace that day, but I remained forever grateful thereafter.

Whenever I lost sight of him ahead, I noted the paw prints leading onward through the soft sand. When I fell too far behind, he paused, waiting just around a bend. Then I would see him in another form, as a Hunter, a man dressed from head to toe in dark gray linens, bound in soft leather. Only his eyes showed through the gap in his headdress, but with the familiar eyes of gold and amber.

At these junctures, Coyote would teach me small things. Many, I realized, I remembered from my training so many years before. Things I had long ago left in the attic of my mind. Things that I never had use of, until now.

During one short break, he led me aside, through a nearly hidden fissure in the rock, an opening I would never have noticed otherwise. Through another ravine, my ears caught the distinct sounds of trickling water.

My first instinct was to rush ahead, to fill my mouth, my belly, my empty canteen. But something in the way he stood to the side, letting me pass, gave me pause. I met his eyes and saw his apprehension at being here with me.

"I am sorry for making you come here, to my rescue."

"Do not apologize, little brother. Two are better equipped to survive than one." The image of the Hunter faded he was back in Coyote form.

"A pack," I mused, and not for the first time, I wondered where his might lie. Why was he a lone hunter out in these wastes?

Before I could ask, he nodded toward the pool just ahead, urging me onward. Dropping to my knees, I looked closely at the crystal-clear water. Then I inhaled,

taking in the faint scent of rotten eggs, sharp and astringent.

"This water is tainted," I muttered, sighing.

Behind me I felt a wave of approval. Inside, my heart sags, feeling defeated all the same.

"To drink it is poison, but it can be a benefit."

Like a hot spring. Minerals are beneficial to the skin. Dipping my hands into the blessedly cool water, I doused my arms, my face. The effect was unbelievably refreshing. I washed my robe, my headdress. But I did not drink, though my mouth begged me to.

When I finished, I felt renewed, though my hunger and thirst remained.

"Come. The way out is nearby."

Placing one foot in front of the other, I trudged on. Soon, my renewed mood deteriorated, exhaustion pulling me down like an anchor. The memories of the night before plagued me. Shadow's words echoed in my thoughts.

"I must rest," I gasped.

"Yes. Soon. But not here."

"I am spent, brother."

"There is always another step. Until there is not."

"So, you say," I grumbled. "It's more than my body. My spirit is tired."

"Those are the troubles of men. For me, there is only the hunt; there is only rest, shelter, food. These are the things that should matter to you in the desert."

"A man has more worries than just that," I say.

"Only what worries you create for yourself. Look at what dangers you brought on in your mind-weary state. You entered the canyon too late. Your supplies were depleted. Your energy is low. You lit a fire with wood. If you had been on the surface, the light and smoke would have been seen for miles. Attracting unwanted attention."

"So, was I to backtrack? To wait to move on?"

"Your priority should always be water. Food. Rest. Time is irrelevant. Distance and progress are irrelevant. Wellness is all. You must learn how to ration your water. How much you need and how to carry more with you if you do not know how to find it. This too, you must learn," Coyote said.

He trotted on ahead, moving with ever greater haste as the sun began to dim.

I lost sight of him for a long while, until suddenly the rock widened around me, revealing a small caldera. In it, my guide sat calmly, sheltered under a darker stone on the far end, a trickle of water pattering over the front of the overhang.

Raising his open mouth to the source, he drank.

All pretense and self-control fled me. Dropping to my hands and knees beneath the rivulets, I gulped down a mouthful. Another. My throat resounded with long-awaited relief. Finally, I sat back, regaining control of myself. Another tenet of the wastes: I would make myself sick filling my gut with water after so long without.

"Seek this type of stone when seeking water," Hunter counseled.

And again, a faint memory surfaced of my studies, the natural purification of groundwater through stones.

After a time, we rose, heading for the path out of the canyon.

"I take it that camping down here is ill advised?"

Coyote replied, "Only if you want to wake up cuddling with a viper."

A chill ran through me at the thought, and I hurried to reach the top before sunset. Just before we crested the trail, Coyote veered off toward an outcropping of rock. In the amber light of late afternoon it sparkled, catching my eye. I became unsure in which form I might find him.

Coyote waited for me to inspect the formation, watching me as he usually did. Waiting for me to make a discovery. Narrowing my eyes, I leaned in, placing my tongue on the white crystals.

"Salt!" I exclaimed; my guide's eyes gleamed with a knowing smile.

Chipping off a few chunks with my knife, I packed them carefully in cloth to keep them dry, tucking a small piece inside my lip. Instantly, I felt a sort of tingle in my brain, an alertness that had been lacking and certainly waning the longer I went without nutrients.

"Come. I have one final reward for your efforts." Coyote led the way, taking a side path that rose up a small mountain.

Though the salt brought with it mental acuity, my body was at its limit. Still, I pressed on, curious what else he might show me.

After a while, Stig broke the silence. "Brother, I must ask. Why have you taken pity on me? You have offered me far more than I have given in return."

"Not so. Your company is more than enough. I have no pack." Coyote reassured.

"Surely there are others you could find."

"Perhaps. For the time being, I chose you. The desert sang to us both, and we met. Our questions were answered with purpose, though we might not understand the nature of her guidance until we part ways," Coyote explained.

I mused, "Purpose. I wonder at times if I will find one. If my journey will bear fruit."

"Has it not already? You came here and you did not die. You respected the sanctity of the desert. You did not try and conquer it but adapted. Neither did you let it conquer you, thus far."

"I was always stubborn," I laughed.

"A trait that bodes well here," Coyote said with a grin.

Behind us and far below, the canyon fell dark, the bright orange disc of the sun dipping low to the horizon. Flickering shadows down in the crags reminded me of my trial, my foe. I knew I was not free of Shadow completely. He nipped at my heels.

So, I sped on, catching up to Hunter as he bent down, looking closely at something.

"Be mindful. Stay present," he murmured, glancing at my eyes and the concern painted clearly there. "Look here. This time of day is best for harvesting."

Following Coyote's gaze, I noted the hive, the buzzing soft and erratic between the rocks.

"Honey?" I wondered, my mouth watering.

"Take only what you need. Do not disturb them too much. They are calm at this hour, the honey warm from the heat of the day," Coyote advised.

Reaching in carefully, I broke off a hunk of the comb, shocked at the sensation of tiny wings against the back of my hand. As I drew the delicate lattice out, a few sleepy bees hovered in its wake, but I received not a single sting.

"Water. Salt. Sugar. These will sustain you between meals."

And without another word, Coyote dropped to all fours, leading the way to a place where I could set camp, a rock shelter overlooking the plains for miles about. Our lessons for the day were at an end.

With no fuel to ignite, we sat close, sharing the sweet nectar, gooey and rich. I have never tasted something so exquisite as the melted gold on my tongue that night. Nor have I savored any meal before or since then as I did that blessing. For the first time in many days, I felt a swell of hope, a spark in my chest. I even acknowledged within myself an eagerness to continue my expedition the next day.

"Now you are prepared to live, not just survive," Coyote mocked, laying down next to me and closing his eyes.

"I would not have even survived without your help, brother," I admitted.

"We may choose to assist one another in the cycle of life, or we will become sustenance in that cycle for another."

"I would rather feed the hearts and souls of others, I think."

"Then you have found meaning."

His words spoke truth to my soul as I drifted off toward my dreams. They grew into a song, whispering out across the horizon, harmonizing with the swish of the sand, the moan of the wind, the cry of the night birds and nocturnal hunters.

Each of them beckoned, asking of the Source. Offering their lives to the cycle. And I felt as one with them.

True to his nature, when I awoke, Coyote was gone. Though chilled, I rose alert and empowered. Though my years would not let me forget the miles I had traveled; strength filled my bones. Lessons I had long forgotten came readily to my mind.

So, I stretched, planting my bare feet to the earth, warming my muscles for the day ahead. From the water, honey, and salt, I formed cakes, drying them on a stone in the sun at midday during my repose.

I set out in the afternoon, spotting a hill in the distance. Climbing it at a leisurely pace, I focused on each flex of my muscles, every twinge, ache and pain. I listened for the first time in a while to the voice of my temple, my body. I gave thanks for my reflexes, my vitality.

When I arrived at the summit of the dune, I basked in great joy and accomplishment for the feat. I grinned as I saw a familiar weathered wagon far below and a leathery hand waving me to join him.

And off in the distance, a trail of smoke slowly rising to the heavens. Lights.

A destination. A purpose.

Stig's Journal, Day 44:

I am never alone, even when I am by myself

I must ask when exploring my existence: what are the needs and the desires of those around me? What does the Creator want? What are my fellows looking for? What do I desire and how does that affect those around me?

Even a selfish man is constantly aware of the people around him. Every action is weighed. So too, the pious man, in how he might serve others, rejecting himself.

Just as the merchant seeks to "find a need and fill it," so should I ask when I interact with anyone else. Myself included. Even more so with the Creator, whose plan for me is written in the stones of the Earth, in my skin and my talents.

I have been blessed to meet some of the most amazing people on planet Earth—soldiers, politicians, entrepreneurs, ministers, scholars, celebrities, and champion athletes.

Each held a universe of potential.

Each a unique and powerful answer to the words "I am . . ."

We become what we believe. The choice is ours.

Prayer

Let me keep my perception outside myself.

In offering aid, I receive many things I need and desire.

Mutual benefit.

Guide me to ask for help, to ask for instruction.

Through the relationships I maintain let me find my calling and how I might offer my service to others. I must ask: How can I give back?

What do I lack that I might ask for humbly?

Have I given thanks for the deeds and gifts given to me, and those that I have to give?

Part 2

Spiritual Healing

Chapter 6

The Dying Oasis

he only way to stay true to new beliefs is to dwell in them and on them. Like a recovering addict, you must surround yourself with others that will hold you accountable to your new life. Who won't let you drop back into your old ways of thinking. Who share your newfound revelations.

This support will cement your foundation in success. Then, it is up to you to pass the same care and service along to others.

Be helped, then help those in need.

Learn from one another. Work together. Change the world.

The telltale signs of an oasis sprouted in my sight a fair way off. Greenery and the scent of water filled the air as I rode along in the back of Peddler's wagon.

We did not speak much on the journey to the town. A simple greeting was exchanged, and I laid down for a nap, ecstatic to be off my feet for a time. When I would wake every so often, I would see Crow, soaring over-head, cheering his cries that I survived.

It brought a smile to my face as I had not known in some time.

In the hours it took for us to arrive, I pondered many things. Digesting all the struggles I had come through by the skin of my teeth was first and foremost. Reality had far outpaced my most vivid imaginings.

But alongside those accomplishments, I ruminated on Coyote's teachings.

As we approached the oasis, it occurred to me that the people who live here might not be friendly, though the Peddler hardly seemed worried. Still, signs of the encroaching desert alerted me to the fact that the oasis was dying, slowly. It clearly had been for many years.

Such conditions could make any citizen hesitant to share resources with an outsider.

They might drive us from town.

Or take what we have and kill us, even.

In harsh conditions, kindness and civilized society shifts quickly when necessities become scarce. Just like the ramshackle buildings on the outskirts of what at one time was likely a hub for trade in this desert. A waypoint.

Now a dour end to a journey.

Not a single voice shouted a greeting, no smiles or glances of interest. The entire place was quiet. As if the inhabitants wanted nothing of what the rest of the world had to offer.

Even so, to me, this place of sparse vegetation and two lagoons that had seen better days, glowed as a marvelous paradise. It was heaven compared to the straits I walked, the carved-out pits I called my bed for weeks on end.

In another life, I would have disdained the piecemeal sheds that clearly someone called home. I would have tolerated such squalor in passing, eager to move on. Instead, I hopped down from the wagon with a grin, waving Peddler on his way. He shouted a farewell with a sly twinkle in his eye before moving on.

A fair way away, he stopped for a time, chatting with another merchant. A man who appeared to have been here some time, hawking his wares. Or rather, from the looks of his cart, trying to.

I turned in a slow circle, drinking in the paltry sights of the place, when a flutter of wings draws my attention. Crow sat atop a building nearby, eyeing me.

"You made it," he clacked.

"All thanks to your diligent eye," I muttered snidely.

"There at last is your sense of humor."

"Nearly dying in the canyon puts things in perspective," I replied.

"As does my view from above," Crow crowed.

"And what insight might you offer?" I asked him.

"Insight equal to whatever tithe you offer in turn."

Ah, yes. I had almost forgotten the nature of the Crow, always willing to help. For a fee. I could not judge him for his nature, and for advice I knew I could trust, no matter the cost. It reminded me of an old acquaintance in my homeland, a merchant who always had the best items, the most useful tips. But always for a reasonable price.

"You certainly deserve these coins I have here. Regardless of what you tell me, I would share them with you." I relented.

Digging into my pouch, I drew out one of the honey cakes, one I specifically made for Crow, one with a crystallized bee trapped in the center of the honey. Crow's eyes lit up.

"For such a treat I tell you this: most keep to themselves in this town. Here you will find the general goods; over there is a tavern. Neither has much to offer. On the edge of town, however, there lies a horde of treasure to be had. No one goes there except to add to the pile," said Crow.

"Thank you, Crow. I will keep these things in mind." True to his summary and a few more directions, I spotted the various buildings, most dilapidated houses with closed shutters or suspicious stares in the windows.

I was shocked at how many souls inhabited the oasis. Less surprising was the lack of a warm welcome.

I knew of other places such as this. Places that attracted those who wished to be left alone. Places where people went when they had given up. More likely to attract vultures than human beings.

An old square marked the center of the village, housing the general goods store butted up against an old tavern.

Both were falling apart, but the tavern looked far less inviting. The street, if it could be considered such, led to the primary watering hole, a pool that had once been much larger. Along its bank, scrawny yet hardy trees swayed lightly in the hot breeze, a few other ferns dotted the shore.

Everywhere else in the town, not a single thing grew. Even so, the sight of anything living made my heart sing. Life persisted in this place. I could too.

Heading into the small store, I blinked in the dimness, the confines of the store stale, but much cooler. My eyes adjusted to reveal the owner, a scowling old man glaring at me as he stood in stooped posture behind the counter, and one other soul in the next room, presumably the tavern.

She sat at a table, playing a game of cards by herself. I took little note of her at the time, noticing only that she was marked with myriad tattoos, looked to have seen many miles of hard road, and she dressed in colorful scarves and sparkling gold jewelry. The game she played looked as if someone else had stood up in the midst of a turn and simply left.

Stepping up to the counter, I purchased a few items I needed that Peddler could not provide. A needle. Thread. The exchange was wordless.

Taking the dried meat I just purchased, along with some bread and cheese Peddler provided, I sat down on the stoop out front. As usual, my meal was simple. Bland.

Compared to the town, however, it was a celebration. A feast.

As I sat and carefully chewed every morsel, my thoughts drifted to my old life. How I once would have considered my provisions paltry, unfit. I had lived a life of decadence. Excess. Never wanting for anything.

Gazing out across the smattering of houses, I considered asking if there was one abandoned that I might claim. Somewhere to cover my head while I explored what purpose I might serve to this community.

For I knew with certainty I was here to serve others, anyone, in any way I could.

Before I could make up my mind whether to head back inside to ask questions of the tight-lipped store clerk, my eyes drooped. Exhaustion pressed against the inside of my lids. I had become accustomed to sleeping during this time of the day, and my body remained synchronized to the ways of the wilderness.

And what a coincidence, that the tavern porch was outfitted with two hammocks, swaying invitingly. Not one to pass up such a welcome, I slipped into the farthest sling, sleep claiming me immediately.

It was a slumber unlike any I had since entering the desert. My mind raced through wild dreams, soaring through open skies and starlit oblivion.

As I spiraled away from the Earth, Crow cackled, flying with me for a time, pointing the way through vibrant galaxies of swirling glory. Though ethereal, it was far more authentic than anything I'd ever experienced in my day-to-day existence. He soared away as I swooped low to the ground, gliding alongside the patter of paws, running in the night.

Coyote smiled at me, and we were one. Isolation waved to me from a mountaintop, a dear friend now. Humility enveloped my wings, filling me with grace and appreciation for what I had.

Then I saw behind the spirits a dark shade and knew that he was near. Shadow. He was kin to Loneliness, brother to foolish Pride.

He was my enemy, and the enemy of peace. The opposite of the pure desert spirit. His presence shattered the quiet embrace of solitude, haunted those who sought succor in service and selflessness.

Just as our eyes met, a jarring crescendo of metal clanged nearby, ringing out across the town, and I nearly tumbled from my hammock. Around the tavern, past a hovel and a shack, I followed the harsh clang of iron clattering against iron. The tumult led me to the edge of the village. To a place I knew Crow spoke of. A scrapyard.

Nearby, another midden heap graced the outskirts, a trove of broken furniture, discarded household goods and other debris. But here . . . in this junkyard, my eyes lit with curiosity.

I began to dig and explore, finding many ancient treasures that only someone who had nothing for several weeks might find any useful. With my satchel near empty of tools, I was able to find several items of note, including an old compass, a spoon, and a metal drinking cup.

Treasures indeed.

With my mind racing and full of newfound possibilities, I envisioned all the things I might build. The mechanical devices I might fix and renew. If only I had tools and a smithy.

In my youth I'd studied under my uncle, a talented blacksmith, apprenticing in the arts of forging. Those memories came alive again, igniting creativity and a desire to make something!

And in answer to my silent request I stumbled on a large metal enclosure, walled in on three sides, filled with every imaginable shape and size of broken wares. All stacked on tables. Workbenches. And in the corner . . . a furnace.

Once, long ago, someone had converted the bottom of an old still into a blacksmith's forge. Repurposed a metal crate into walls and a roof. An anvil hid under a canvas tarp. Along one wall a rusted cabinet held hammers and tongs.

Excitement thrilled me, sending me into a frenzy as I cleared the mess away, unveiling a workshop. Childlike wonder overflowed.

Soon, a line of usable metal lined one wall, material for making knives, an idea forming to perfect my crude desert weapon. To provide expert tools for those in this town, and further, to share my creations with the world someday.

Of course, I knew I was getting far ahead of myself. However, I had not felt such elation in so long. I felt driven by a compulsion to act and express that side of me I had not explored in many years. A nearly extinguished ember was sparking wastes back to life.

With food available, a shelter over my head, and weeks of introspection, I needed a task.

Without a thought, I stoked the forge, hammering through the afternoon without a thought to the noise or the heat. I drank when needed, washed my face in the lagoon.

Each of these I fixated on, immersed in the present. The exertion of hammering nurtured my masculine nature.

So lost was I in my work, that I almost did not notice I was being watched.

A presence at the edge of the scrapyard, moving closer. The flash of bright color catches my eye finally and I pause, looking to find the tattooed woman from the tavern.

She puttered along as if she belonged in this place, seemingly oblivious to me. Age barely bent her back, and her features I must confess, were quite striking. Despite the years, her dark brown eyes gleamed, reminding me of Peddler.

Clearly, she was once a great beauty and still wore the trappings of a once wealthy woman. Gold. Bright silk. She hummed pleasantly in her passing, ignoring me completely.

With a huff and a sniff, she kicked over a pile of refuse, muttering about needing to clean up.

For some reason, I stood silent and still, watching her for a time. Honestly, I was stunned.

Finally, she half turned after inspecting the whole of the yard and sighed.

"No one. Not a soul."

"I beg your pardon, mistress?" The sound of my own voice sang strangely in my ears.

"No one has stepped foot in this place in decades." She waved one hand around her in explanation. "This place has not known sound or fire in years. Creation gave way to ruin. Yet here you are, stoking the fires, bringing life back to a dying land."

"I could not help myself. I felt drawn here."

"As I am sure you were called to enter the desert. Many of us were at one time, too."

"Do you think anyone will mind?" I asked.

"I do not mind, and that is all that matters," she snapped, smirking at me. "Everything you see on this side of town is mine."

"You live here?"

"No. Once, I did. Now I only return to check on the state of this place. A memory fading. Much like me."

I found her candid words appealing, her blunt nature charming.

"You are radiant, still," I acknowledged.

"You are a grifter! I know my looks have abandoned me." Still, she hid a smile.

"What do I call you, mistress?"

"Sage will do."

"Then I ask, Sage, may I stay and work this forge for a time? I will contribute. I would even pay."

The elder woman faced me then, and I saw it; the authority and pride emanating from within her. A motherly power radiated from her; a sadness wrapped about her shoulders like her shawl. This was a Matron of the world, a keeper of truth and great wisdom.

"If there were a tribute to be paid, I would accept it. But alas, I came here to part with this land. Even so, I think it would be lovely to have the company of a handsome young man."

"Thank you, Sage."

She turned away, waving over her shoulder.

At the edge of the yard, Sage called back, "On one condition, that you sit and speak with me, play games with me in the heat of the day."

"I would be honored."

Stig's Journal, Day 50

Give and be given to. Earth Angels are real.

They wander the land, keeping their eyes open for opportunities to change lives. Any of us can take that form at any time. So, I must remain alert.

Coyote came to my rescue in the night, in my darkest hour.

The Peddler arrived at the most opportune time to lift my spirits and offer me a ride. Serendipity? I think not.

After completing a trial and facing my fears, being nearly forced to accept assistance, no salvation, offered by a friend, I needed the relief of finding a triumph within my reach. The town on the horizon marked the end of one stage of my journey, and the start of another.

I must take signs like these as gestures of Love from the Source.

God is good, merciful, and forgiving. The Universe is benevolent and wants the best for all of us.

Suffering can be a gift. Embrace every struggle with joy. Learn and grow.

Be wary of your limits. Too much suffering will eventually break you down. These are the times when we must open our hearts and eyes to the Earth Angels around us.

Prayer

Lift the veil from my eyes that blinds me to opportunity.

I long to exchange ideas and share with great minds like mine.

On this path, how can I be proactive?

What are my responsibilities toward others?

Toward God? Toward myself?

Where am I failing in showing up with presence, and delivering what I promise?

What consequences have I suffered for my errors? How do I prevent them from occurring again?

Who will I choose to be accountable to?

Chapter 7

The Scrapyard

E very hero's journey looks different, but we all should endeavor to set out on one at least once in our lives. Some people travel to Spain on a walking pilgrimage. Others seek Mecca in their own way, either the city or what it represents.

Each belief varies in their procedure, but all seek a higher knowledge of spiritual intelligence.

Some, like me, must travel to the valley of death, while others take their journeys quietly in their own home, at a local church, temple, synagogue, or counseling.

I myself took several journeys throughout my life. A hard learner I have always been.

The result, however, was always a shift in my entire worldview.

My return to a semblance of civilization saw a return of some old routines and habits, not all of them bad. Having daily tasks, a schedule of sorts, did wonders for my mood and positivity.

Structure can be a hearty foundation for rebuilding and rediscovering passions and skills.

I cleaned the smithy, organized the scrapyard into a usable state.

The hard work cleared my head and strengthened my body.

Guaranteed sustenance waiting for me after hard labor encouraged giving my all, helping me find my center once more.

Ordering and tidying my workspace served to clear the clutter out of my thoughts, as well. Two days of rigorous cleaning saw the place looking unrecognizable when Sage stopped by again to check on me and bring me a waterskin and some freshly baked bread.

"My, my, what a stunning sight," she marveled, giving me a look.

I smiled, catching her jest as I wiped sweat from my bare chest. Such was her way, keeping me off guard with a joke, often flirting with me. The comments were always innocent and well-intended.

"Thank you, I only wished to repay you for your kindness by setting the yard in good standing." I smiled.

"You certainly turned this place around. A fresh face in these parts would have been enough, but I am impressed," Sage admitted.

"Please, if there are any other tasks you require, I am happy to assist."

"Well, now that you mention it, I could use your help carrying water from the well."

"I would be more than happy to."

"Later, though. You are clearly in the middle of crafting a fine piece of workmanship there!" She appraised the knife blade resting on the anvil's surface, my best one yet.

"I have only begun to regain my skill with the hammer," I humbly replied.

But she was not wrong.

The pieces I had completed so far were quite good. A few of the townsfolk stopped by, commenting on the quality of my work. It seemed my craftsmanship had earned their respect. Then I offered to fix any items they might need repaired, and I got my first customers.

I mended a hammer for the cobbler, patched a pail and a shovel for an elderly woman who kept an herb and vegetable garden near the lagoon, and several other odds and ends. The best part was the simple exchange, serving others in ways that truly benefited them.

In payment, I only asked that they bring me a cooked meal every now and again, if I accepted payment at all. After all, the materials in the scrapyard belonged to Sage, or were broken from piles of refuse and junk.

With those jobs complete, I returned to my blade smithing, honing and refining my methods. It had been decades since I worked with metal, but the smell and the feel of the craft lived in my muscles' memories. My hand-eye coordination had gratefully not fallen prey to the piling up of years.

Ever since I was a youth, I had a knack for creating things. Converting one thing into another held a unique satisfaction for me, particularly items that could be put to technical or mechanical use.

And through the work, I gained a solitary goal, a repetitive practice. That sort of simple effort promotes peace that many people, me included, lack in the hustle of daily life.

Hours alone in the shop gave me perspective and much time to ponder any and all things.

My frustration with my old life, the rut I felt I had fallen into, looked so different from this distance. I recalled the requests of those beneath my employ who sought guidance, my kin and acquaintances begging solutions to questions I did not feel I had the time to answer, decisions and judgments regarding quarrels that meant nothing to me.

And I saw them for what they were.

The importance of each and every person's own experiences was everything to them, just as my own issues seemed of the utmost importance to me.

Serving the simple needs of the oasis-folk allowed me to understand them, thereby allowing me to better serve them. And in doing so, grow in compassion, understanding and grace.

After so many years on this Earth, it was an easy thing to forget that one never stops learning, never stops evolving.

That said, a man does not simply wander into the desert for no reason. I had indeed come here to discover these great lessons again and new lessons, too.

Such as the way a place can feel like home, even knowing that my time there would be short.

Hours spent in close conversation with Sage, playing her board games and card games reminded me of family and the warmth of a hearth. Long afternoons spent with an old man whose name I never learned on the porch of the tavern, laying in a hammock in quiet company filled my soul.

These were special days I would always treasure, but far from the culmination of my time in the wastelands. That epiphany was yet to come.

So it was that I stood at my smithy, hammering away on a particularly tricky edge of a blade, drawing out the full tang of the knife that would extend through the handle, when Peddler passed my way.

Leaving his wagon at the sorry excuse for a stable, he strode right up to my table, winking at me with those bright eyes. I continued about my business as he browsed the blades on display there.

"Ah, Stig! Or perhaps no longer. I see you have been put to work."

"Hardly, Peddler, my friend. I found this work waiting for me and eager to be completed!" I grinned as I tugged down my bandana.

"You are not one to remain idle, then."

"Something I know you can relate to. Neither of us have lost the youth in our souls," I replied.

"Only in our backs and bones!" He smirked, the wrinkles of his face crinkling.

As weathered as that face appeared, Peddler's stature, his stance, and his nimbleness belied a man half his age. I hoped that I might remain in such health at his age. Yet what struck me most whenever I encountered him, was the nature of his spirit, as old as the Earth itself, older perhaps. A timelessness to his character and presence that instilled a wonder within me.

Had he wandered these lands since the beginning of time?

Indeed, he had. For someone like him had always assumed his role, an archetype like many others I've met throughout my life. That is the eternity in our humanity. Roles we embody that echo through history.

That was not the time to muse on such universal thoughts, however. The Peddler clearly came as a customer. His discerning eye fell on the two bests of my stock, twinkling with interest.

"These are quite fine," he said, tapping his bearded chin. "I am in need of a new blade. Mine is old, chipped and dull."

"You are welcome to anything you see, Peddler. I could never repay you for your kindness and generosity to me."

"Nonsense. We are of a kind, you and me. You would not simply take without paying what is due."

Though he was correct, I had always compensated him for his wares, I nevertheless could not bring myself to put a price on anything I made.

"Everything you see came from scrap in this heap. The owner, Sage, told me that anything I create with it, I am free to do with as I please."

"Then if it pleases you, I will not take a man's hard work for free, especially of such quality," the Peddler persuaded.

"Fine," I conceded, knowing the argument was futile. "Choose one, and I will give you a good price on it. However, I insist that you allow me to repair your old blade. Rusty though it may be, it might still serve you well with a bit of attention."

"Fair enough. No sense in adding to this scrap pile!"

"Indeed. Never cast aside a tool that holds the potential of work unfinished," I added.

"Now those are words of wisdom," he muttered, choosing his knife, "Yet here you are . . ."

I wondered at the way he said it, how he meant it. I certainly had thrown myself away many times, straying from my purpose and calling. Was I straying now?

Losing myself in a distraction instead of finding the voice in the desert?

Casting those ideas aside, I set to sharpening Peddler's old blade.

He purchased the best of my stock, one for himself, another as a gift. We shook hands and he went on his way.

Later in the day, his wagon clattered past my shop, headed out into the wastes again to the southwest. Movement caught my eye behind him as he passed the last patch of brush.

Loping along in his wake, I almost mistook the creature for my companion.

I had not seen Coyote much since I arrived in town, with good reason. He had no use for domestication. Still, in the evening, I would walk to the edge of the village to share a bowl of water and a bit of meat with him when I could.

This creature, however, was tawny, skinny and doing a poor job of staying out of sight. Drawing out one of my treasured finds in the yard, I placed the seeing glass to my eye.

And saw the lion for what it was, stalking the Peddler's wagon.

Immediately, I rushed out, cutting a path around and across the dunes to intercept my friend. Waving my arms, I signaled him quietly to stop. Reaching him in a huff, I pointed back the way he had come, drawing my knife to warn him of danger.

Peddler smiled, raising one hand in peace.

"There is a young lion of the mountains chasing you, Peddler. Turn around and return to the safety of town, at least for the night."

"Are you so sure? Look again."

And I did. The beast appeared scared, its ribs showing through its skin.

"Do you see? He is desperate."

"Indeed. This lion does not prowl. He barely knows how. Which means he has not learned the ways of the pride."

"Then what does he seek?"

"Observe the way he stands, the look in his eyes. He hungers, yes. But not just for food. He seeks something else. Instruction. Assistance. Survival."

I saw the truth in Peddler's words and felt a kinship with the state of the lion. He mirrored a version of myself from only a few weeks prior. Searching. Lost. Yet proud. Determined.

"Consider, Stig, perhaps the young lion could use someone who recently learned their own lessons of the desert. Knowledge of the land to better help him in his way, to help him become a great lion."

Locking eyes with the young animal, my chest swelled with emotion. And a need to offer care to this lonely youth.

So, I took another step in my journey

Stig's Journal, Day 53

I am as I present myself.

There is nothing quite like being seen for who you are. Certain people in your life will naturally notice your talents, your true nature.

Outside of those few, one must decide how they want to be seen.

Finding myself in the presence of others again made me analyze how they viewed me. As an outsider, the burden of making a good impression laid with me. Even more so with such distrusting and solitary folk as those that lived in the oasis.

Vending my services and wares put the encounters in a unique perspective for me.

I needed to position myself in a favorable light. My wares and my approachability relied on a branding of sorts, something they would be attracted to and were familiar with. Learning how to discern the expectations of others proved to be one of my greatest assets.

Especially when I met a young lion, who saw me as a threat, a stranger, but a potential ally.

Prayer

How do you see me, great Source of all life?

I desire to stand as an icon of ingenuousness, transparent to anyone I meet. Let them see who I am, let my qualities and character be clear and visible.

I will ask daily to remain forthright and true.

I will ask myself difficult questions that challenge my spirit.

How well am I doing as a protector and a provider?

Am I an anchoring point of safety for others, or an anchor that drags them down?

Chapter 8
The Lion

*Y*oung men hunger for a "hero's journey," especially those who lacked a father figure. I had many, yet I still craved adventure, knowledge, creativity. We all must feed our warrior soul.

As such, we must seek our journey, our vision quest alone in nature, seeking God's will. Sometimes we must undergo many of these endeavors throughout our lives. The end result, the goal, is to create better men and better women for a better world.

Find a place in your life and among people who challenge you. A place to laugh, learn, cry, and grow. A place where iron sharpens iron. Find honor, respect, self-discipline.

I prayed in the desert for reflection and inspiration. I sang. I told tales and shared the secrets of my soul. All in the pursuit of fulfilling my need to be a provider, protector, and a procurator for the world.

This is the contract we must make with ourselves, a contract signed in our own blood.

A covenant.

"You must stay downwind, young lion, to get the drop on your prey. Staying out of sight is one thing, not being heard, another entirely," I whispered, crouching low in the sparse grass.

"I am invisible. They cannot see me, or hear me," he replied.

"So, you think. But more than that, do you not smell your prey? You sense them nearby. They have been designed by the universe to sense you coming, to smell you coming, and to react to danger. Their instincts are strong, so your instincts must be even more powerful."

"But I am hungry, and stronger."

"You are strong. However, they are fast. If you do not use every advantage at your disposal, you will soon be hungry and weak. You must let nature guide you."

The lion grumbled softly, scowling. "Teach me."

"Use the breeze to detect the angle of your attack. Always approach from downwind."

"And when there is no breeze?"

"You must learn patience."

"Patience sounds a lot like being hungry."

"Self-control is everything, young one. Once you master that, you will make fewer mistakes. Then you will be able to provide for yourself and your family, your tribe." As usual, the mention of the lion's pride brought a shadow of sadness, but he nodded, paying heed to my words.

The first several days of his stay with me started tense and confrontational. His lessons in the ways of the desert even more so. He was not prone to listen and prone to aggression, to arguing with me, to fighting back, to doing it his way.

Until he lost several rabbits and a wayward deer. The inherent pride in his nature was taking a thrashing. I recognized it as his opportunity for a breakthrough. I navigated his frustration carefully, and soon, he began to ask questions, to actually listen to my answers. A wound to his pride and confidence could be extremely detrimental to his growth, yet he needed to become the master of his faculties if he was to become an adult lion and a powerful male of his species.

Such is the balance of being a strong man.

Guiding, instructing, but always remaining in control. Listening and responding with steadfast discipline. Centering the lessons in kindness, even when reprimanding.

So too, the way of the leader.

"A leader is proud, but his pride does not govern him." I told him.

"I do not understand."

"There, a hare. Take it and I will show you."

The lion's eyes flashed; he darted from cover, circling naturally, hemming the unsuspecting long-ear. Ears twitched; the creature bolted.

But Lion was clever.

He used the arch of the surrounding rocks not only to throw off the sound of his approach but to block his prey in.

The kill should have been quick.

Lion whooped with glee, pouncing one way, then another. Bounding forward, he taunted the animal with the chance of escape before cutting him off again. Finally, after a few more attempts, Lion finished him off.

And just as I knew he would, Lion loped back to me, the hare in the grin of his teeth.

Dropping the kill at my feet, he preened. "Ha! I learn well, do I not?"

"You learned some," I snapped crossly.

A flare of anger narrowed Lion's eyes. "Why do you shame my success? You are just jealous."

"I am not jealous of childish antics."

The statement widened his eyes with concern. This was the line where I had to tread carefully.

Sighing, I patted him on the back, gesturing that he should eat his meal. He slumped to the dirt, dejected.

"Do not pout. I am pleased with your success. However, the means of your success bothers me."

Lion tore at the hare, frowning in thought. "I should not have toyed with it."

"No, you shouldn't have. It is one thing to revel in the thrill of the chase. Such is your nature. Using your skill should be applauded. Enjoyed, even."

"Is that why it tastes bad?" Lion asked.

"Perhaps. Fear is natural. Despair in the face of torture is cruel."

"I am sorry." He dropped his head.

"Do not say you are sorry. Say you will be better."

"I will," Lion agreed.

So many lessons. Many of them came back to me in the process of teaching this cub hard earned lessons from my own youth. Ideals ingrained into me by my father, my grandfather, and my teachers. Some were painful memories once, shame of failure filled with words of scorn.

Thus, I tempered them with my own experience, removing the harsh sting of my father's sneer. He had a way of cutting deep.

In that way, he still taught me how I would be different as a mentor.

Once trust grew between us, we traveled as comrades across the landscape each day. I showed the young lion which plants were safe to eat, which ones would cause him to vomit purposely if he became ill, and how to find water. Just like the coyote showed me, I shared my knowledge and wisdom with Lion.

They say teaching instructs the teacher as much as the student.

So, I learned truly how to respect the desert in all her ways. Often, Crow joined us, guiding us to good hunting, to water when we lost our way. In that way I taught the Lion the benefit of a pack.

"Why do you do that?" Lion tilted his furry head as we sat beside my nightly fire in the scrapyard. Opening my eyes, I took a bite of my evening meal.

"I give thanks for the food I take from the land. The bounty of life."

"Why? You hunted the meat. You cooked it." He grimaced as he said it, still appalled at the way I "ruined" what he considered perfectly good eating.

"I give thanks to the spirit of the animal for lending life to me. I show gratitude to the universe that I am able to survive another day. The Source supplies all of this abundance to the world. When we partake of that offering, we must be wary of the balance."

"Men take too much. I have seen them on the edges of the desert," Lion explained.

"Yes. Many do. They are greedy. This puts the Earth out of balance," I agreed.

"So, it is wrong to take what I need?"

"No, young one." I stared for a time into the fire, thinking of how to explain. "It is not a matter of who is better, who is more deserving. When a true sacrifice is made, it is for the benefit of others. You may find that you make a sacrifice of your own someday."

He listened well, but I feared he did not understand. How was I to tell him, to show him the lesson most dear to my heart. The one that I still struggled with even then.

"I frequently ignored the wisdom and teachings of my elders, thinking myself smarter, wiser. Youthful

energy turned into brazen anger. Bitterness. I learned that the part of me that was aggressive was wrong. It was a lie that poisoned me then. My masculinity appeared to be something to be subdued, even eliminated."

"But if it was part of your nature, how could it be so wrong?" Lion asked.

"That is the key. Steel must be tempered, forged into a tool. A knife, like the ones I create in the smithy, for example."

"Sort of like how you said that you need the right tool for the right job?"

"Precisely!" I smiled. "Fostering your masculinity and your boldness and learning to master them will make you able to lend those strengths to others."

We slept well that night, dreaming peaceful dreams of the hunt.

Yet in the days that followed, a troublesome itch still lingered in my mind. Instilling character and lessons of truth also revealed my own memories of failure and remorse. I could use those hard lessons to help Lion avoid my mistakes, but many of them I realized, I had not dealt with personally.

Too many friends left without apologies when I wronged them.

Words spoken in anger toward family.

I blamed my temper, the natural prowess of my strong personality. The desert revealed to me how foolish those excuses were. Every time I focused on myself,

I denied my true purpose in a misguided effort to feed my own hubris.

Humans' place in the cosmos is directly related to their image of God.

For much of my life, even throughout my religious and spiritual studies, I remained the focus of my concern. Me. Myself.

Our struggles can truly blind us to humility and the simple fact that we all suffer the same trials within. In teaching the young lion, I found a bit of healing for many of those old wounds.

"Tell me, Stig," Lion asked as we walked along the bank of the oasis lagoon one morning, "You speak sometimes of God, or of the Source..."

"Yes. Some say Creator, others Mother Earth. Many struggle with proof that a higher being exists."

"Existence is proof enough of a Great Provider."

I grinned, nodding my approval of his inherent wisdom. "Each individual sees this force in the universe in his or her own way. For me, He is all of this around us: water, sand, air. He is the Father and the Mother of all. Most importantly, I believe He exists within us all."

"Yes," said the lion, "In small ways. Like when we find water unexpectedly!"

"That is a perfect example. So too, the design of the desert flowers, the way the insects pollinate and cultivate the plant life. A perfect spider web, a geometric honeycomb. We are all put together, blood and bone and vein, spirit and a spark of life."

In that way, I felt that I conveyed my idea well, as Lion sat with a twinkle in his eye, the ember of a new thought. Inspiration and understanding.

I felt that way many times in life and reveled in it as I showed this young creature the ways of the world. The doubts and misgivings that haunted me through the desert, I kept to myself, not wanting to poison the young mind with Shadow.

The following day, Peddler arrived again in the oasis, finding the two of us out under a palm tree during the hottest hours of the day. There, Lion recounted our lessons, displaying his impressive knowledge and glowing with accomplishment. Truly, he was transformed even after only a few days of careful instruction.

"Indeed, you should be proud, both of you. The wisest lion learns from the teachings of the old ones, without having to make as many mistakes for themselves. True ingenuity comes from building on lessons to achieve greater goals. At times we all need to touch the hot griddle to understand that fire burns but heeding the warnings of those you trust can save you so much grief," Peddler summarized, his eyes gleaming mischievously.

Lion showed his fangs in a grin, nodding. "Experience is the best teacher, and I had one with a lifetime of experience."

"Ha! And he's clever, to boot." Peddler chuckled. We talked and laughed together as friends that day, long into the evening, and I knew our time was coming to an end. Early the next morning, Lion nudged me awake. "Teacher, I feel I am ready to set out on my own to find my tribe again."

"I trust your assessment. And I agree," I said sadly, yet hopeful as I pressed my forehead to his.

The Peddler and I saw him off before the sun rose. "What will your purpose be, young one? What will you seek to accomplish when you return to your pride?" I asked.

"I have thought long and hard on this, Stig. I believe that I would serve them best as a teacher in my own right. Not to challenge the king again, or take his place, but to support him and help our pride thrive."

"There is nothing more for me to teach you."

Peddler patted me on the back, the two of us content to watch the lithe, graceful creature bound off across the early morning blue-hued sand. We shared more than a single tear, and a healing silence that spoke to me, whispering of a time to come when I would face silence and solitude in my own way.

"I must be going, Stig. But think now on this experience and tell me when next we cross paths: what lessons did you take from the lion? What did you learn about yourself from teaching another?"

Many answers bubbled to the surface of my mind, but none of them felt complete or true. So, I said nothing.

When I turned back towards town, the Peddler was gone, in the fashion that he often was, and I found myself

alone in the darkness, following our footsteps back to the scrapyard.

And as it so often happens following an achievement, all the doubts and the worst memories of my past surfaced in my wake, tearing my confidence to shreds despite my success in teaching Lion. Shadow crept along at my back, matching me step for step and I could not shake him.

The dark dreams found me again, this time, in my new home.

Stig's Journal, Day 60

Teach me as I teach.

Fostering skill and pride as a mentor bolstered my spirits. How long has it been since I shared my knowledge and experience with another? How long since I benefited from a receptive pupil?

The soldier does not stand alone. Otherwise, he is only a fighter. A lone man battling without orders. A warrior can be part of a team, but must and will take proactive independent initiative.

Young men need guidance. If they do not receive it, they become old men set in wounded ways, too proud to change. Together, men can grow. This is a metaphor for fellowship, community.

But be careful of the people you surround yourself with.

Wicked men will warp your desires, make you wicked like them.

Holy men will uplift you, encourage you. These are the soldiers you need at your side. Warriors of the spirit who want to heal, and to help you heal.

Leading another through trials you have overcome is the purest form of affirmation.

Prayer

Guide me, teach me to recognize the right path. If I stay on my current path, where will I end up?

Is that what I want?

What insecurities do I deny and suppress?

How can I bring them to the light?

To those friends who bring me down, and the ones who lift me up,

what would I say to them now?

Gratitude? To ask or offer forgiveness?

What specifically do I need to say or ask to heal and grow for the issue troubling me now?

Chapter 9
The Sage

To discover our life's calling, we start with the needs of others. Then our gifts. Then our passions. All of these things must be tied back into the center, the Divine that gifted us life and talent, love and hardship.

From there, we can address the struggles, the frustrations, the wounds. Obstacles and injury hinder our fulfillment. We must heal them to seize our true destiny. With that intellectual plan we must overlay the spirit, stepping into our roles and be validated by the Source, the Divine.

Only then will those gifts, desires, and needs be met with overwhelming bountiful blessings.

We will stumble and fall along the way.

Just as the prophet Hosea listened to God and married a prostitute, offering redemption and a new life. She failed him, ran from him, betrayed him with other men. Yet he welcomed his wife with forgiveness, grace, and mercy.

Through forgiveness we find another chance to achieve our purpose.

It was during my time at the oasis with Sage that mysteries would be unlocked—ones I could not yet fathom.

"Not that I mind, Sage, but why am I always the one to make the tea?" I shuffled about her small kitchen, well acquainted after many afternoons spent conversing and sharing meals.

"Because I have made the tea so many times for others. And you are generous and kind," the older woman said, smiling. Softly, under her breath, she laughed the way she always did.

"You have earned a respite from playing hostess, then," I agreed, pouring each of us a cup.

"In every way one might do so." She raised her eyebrows as she said it, a suggestive comment about her past. "And besides, I like watching you make it. Almost as much as I enjoy watching you hammer away at your anvil. Being served by a good-looking young man is a treat I would not pass up."

"Only once a warrior-man has been through hell can he make a great cup of tea. But I am hardly young, Sage."

"Compared to me, everyone is young. My years are tenfold for my experiences lived."

I joined her in a laugh as I took my seat, laying out a plate of cakes and bread. The food was simple, as all things in the oasis—simple, but fulfilling.

"And I am honored to be graced with the presence of a woman of such beauty."

"Flattery! Careful of the ground on which you tread, boy. You might find yourself in sinking sand, trapped forever by my wiles." She tossed back her hair and winked.

"One wonders why such a rare jewel has not already ensnared a fellow?" I asked.

"Ah. But I have. Two great loves among the many minor seekers and suitors. Both of them now passed."

"Then you are blessed, and then some."

"I certainly was. With great beauty! You should have seen me in my prime, a courtesan of the highest renown. A rare jewel indeed. Men traveled for miles but to lay their eyes on my visage." She closed her eyes then, tilting her head as if to preen and pose.

"Yet you remain ever humble," I mused, hiding my smile.

"When your great works have passed, when the vibrancy fades, you revel in those deeds. Otherwise, you wither in bitterness of loss."

This I understood well. Such feelings had driven me from my home where I was considered a good man, righteous in my own mind and practices. In my youth, I followed the book of the law, the words of God—strictly, rigorously. Even when I questioned and rebelled, I did so in frustration of these rules. As an adult, I remained steadfast to this belief, not necessarily understanding why I chose to do so.

It was a system to follow. A structure. And I was proud to employ it so vehemently.

But why did I believe it? How did my beliefs affect my actions?

Without context, failures and obstacles become questions of doubt.

Is a terrible occurrence our fault? Punishment?

Our guilt manifests in the world around us. I shared some of these thoughts with her in those days. She was, among other things, an excellent listener.

"You are wise, Sage. Would that I understood such ways of love and the fairer sex. My pursuits led me elsewhere. Eventually I accepted that a partner, at least a lifelong one, was not for me."

"And so, you indulged, did you not? This is the easy path of a wayward man. I met many in my years serving them, even more once I guided girls of my own in the ways of pleasure."

At times her candid and open nature seemed abrasive to me.

Yet, something in the accepting and gracious manner in which she conducted herself spoke deeply to me. Such was her lesson, in act and word. And I chose to learn it as best I could.

She had once been a dancer, a concubine, and then a madam to women like herself.

When I first heard this, of course, I quite promptly put my foot in my mouth.

Thank the Maker that she did not easily offend.

"Beauty is a gift, to be enjoyed. So, yes. I pursued beauty, as many men do."

Her eyes bore into mine. "And you found the hollowness that comes from superficial relationships, I am sure. But you never found a true beauty, the kind that comes from within."

I contemplated for a moment. "Perhaps that is the lesson I came here to learn?"

"One of many," she muttered, smiling conspiratorially. "First, you must come to find your own beauty."

"Indeed. Seeking that fulfillment outside myself only bred resentment when I could not find it."

"Ah, yes. Such feelings breed an immature soul, which in turn may lead to sexual sin, deviance. The betrayal of your own spirit. Many throw themselves away in this fashion."

Sage sipped her steaming cup of tea as I considered her words.

As forward as I thought of myself, having this sort of conversation with a woman often felt controversial. However, I craved the knowledge that someone of her learning and wisdom might offer. So, I did not pass up an opportunity to pry into the ways of the female heart.

She interrupted my thoughts. "Tell me, why have you remained unmarried, Stig?"

"I told you, the chances which knocked never felt . . . right."

"Do you lie to yourself often?"

I nearly spit my tea at the expression on her face and the way she cut to the quick.

"I admit, these things always eluded me. The mysteries of women, the way their mind works, always fascinated me," I confessed.

"And why shouldn't they? A mystery is a quest to be solved, certainly. Who better to solve it than a virile, confident man?" Sage suggested.

"Keeping company of the fairer sex pleased me greatly. Dancing, conversing. What drove me to those same encounters was what also drove me away. I have always longed for true love, but more than that, I longed for purpose."

"Then your soul was wise to begin with. Purpose within must come first. Have you thought that instead of failing to find your mate, you were merely unprepared to be 'the one' for someone else?" She waited for a response.

This mirror image struck me deeply. That I was not ready, not for my own sake, but for a perfect pairing yet to come.

Still, too many years had passed. Too many scars resided on my skin.

Sage continued, "Oh, don't look so down. You are a

strapping fellow! Although, it is a shame that you never bore sons. You would have made a great father."

To this I smiled truly. "I have fathered young men, soldiers, brothers. In my own way."

"Careful, you're starting to sound like me."

"Are you not a mother to those here in the desert? You provide guidance, provision, a place to stay for those in need. By your own words, you need not have children of your own to mother those around you." My logic seemed indisputable.

"Who is giving the lessons here? And I never said I did not bear children of my own. They are all gone, out in the world on their way, or to the great beyond."

"I am sorry to hear that, Mother," the words slipped from my mouth.

Sage stared at me for a time, blushing slightly. Then a brilliant smile spread across her face. There, a hint of that unparalleled beauty glowed still, and I found myself charmed. Not in an untoward way. Only as one admires a great work of art.

Here she was, mother, wife, daughter, sister. All roles of femininity expressed in their own time. She was grandmother serving me tea, offering wisdom. A hostess, a comforter, a medicine woman of the soul. Any attraction I felt was the longing to know her spirit and mind, to understand the unknowable magic of a woman's existence.

She told me a great many things, treasures of how to

speak to a woman, how to treat her, and even the secret arts of lovemaking. To this day, no greater knowledge has been bestowed on me. Such insights changed the way I approached friend and partner alike.

"Stig, you are a very rugged yet elegant man, a man with deep caring, compassion and empathy; a wild almost savage man and a sinner, yet also a man of deep faith and a personal relationship with and deep love for God like no other I have ever seen. Decidedly unconventional, yet authentic, sincere and beautiful," she said. "I spent years working with masters, to heal my own wounds so that I could help others heal theirs. I learned to recognize patterns. You still have some demon stuck in you. You manage it surprisingly well, but I will help you to pray and drive it out. It is a ritual I will do for you before you're allowed to touch me."

She helped me understand that she needed to meet me in my darkness first, to dispel the gloom and bring me fully into the light.

As we continued to explore life's intricacies even more deeply, she revealed things that to some extent I already knew, but only intellectually. I never before knew them in my heart. Erotica, she explained, is a powerful and mysterious force with an undeniable energy—but only in its rightful time and place. For the first time in my life, I came to realize that both women and men everywhere are suffering needlessly because they fail to grasp the

vital reality that sex is indeed sacred—that romance and sacred sex are the best path forward.

Sage expressed herself with an empathy I found enchanting. "You too, just like me, and likely millions of people around the world, especially women, have similar childhood trauma . . . and still live with the consequences of that. You have healed well but your inner child is still vulnerable. I have ways to heal this brokenness."

I marveled at her insights and listened with rapt attention to her every word.

"Though sad and tragic, childhood emotional and sexual trauma as well as your adult wounds can lead to tremendous growth. It is what makes you so keenly aware that many have a problem. It is what makes you care, fanning the flames of your authentic compassion and empathy."

She paused for a moment before she continued. "Many women grew up with absent fathers, or emotionally cold mothers, and they suffer alone in deep loneliness. Many suffer from spiritual weakness, sexual wounds and a deep inner void. They need help."

I grew even more intrigued. "Your words have touched my soul," I said.

With a knowing smile, Sage said, "I'm willing to teach you the path to spiritual wholeness, and sexual healing. If you choose this path then our collective mission is to help restore the world to wholeness. And that starts with spiritual wholeness, which is closely interconnected with sexual wholeness.

In all my many relationships with women over the years, though I tried to be a sensitive and caring man. I'd never processed the kinds of insights I was now absorbing like a sponge. This wasn't just some sort of lecture or discourse, it was a life-changing revelation that even at that very moment I realized would profoundly impact not only my own future, but that of countless others.

She looked at me with the utmost sincerity. "You could be of wonderful service to humanity, Stig," she said, "teaching women how to restore sexuality to a more sacred experience and how to renew spiritually and heal sexually. You can, if you're willing, show them how to regain their sweetness of spirit, how to attract and manifest their dream partner, and the three things to make their men obsessed with them and never want to cheat on them, nor leave and abandon them."

She helped me to understand that women today live under tremendous stress and are in deep need of this all-natural stress relief system for optimal mental, emotional and spiritual sexual wellness. Far too many women, and men, suffer from fear, guilt, shame, denial, repression, abuse, harsh uncaring ignorant judgment and much more. Far too many are deeply lonely, under-loved, and under-touched causing mental-emotional problems. The deepest root cause is always foremost spiritual. Only then mental-emotional-sexual.

Sage implored me, "Bring awareness to them, and teach their partners the secret, sacred, how-to protocol I am about to reveal to you. Maybe I will even let you practice on me to master the protocol."

That evening, in the still of the night, under a full moon she revealed the most sacred, honoring of women, potent, and nurturing ritual I had ever witnessed. She said, "Give it as a gift, with zero expectations of any sexual reciprocity in return."

As we continued our precious time together, she talked about and showed me ancient secrets and sacred cleansing practices. How to pray, set sacred intentions, and create a safe, sacred, tidy, and beautiful space—a holy space.

Sage, the wise older woman, stressed the importance of prayer, meditation, purification, breathing, holy oil anointing, and truly caring communication—apologizing and asking for permission, speaking the seven-fold blessing, asking permission and more, including the importance of sincere gratitude.

She put me though an intense ordeal, to be purified, nurtured and healed though prayer, and a hands-on process for men. She taught me hands-on the sacred one and two hand positions, hand motions, and the sacred pressure points, and the secret sacred numerical code—a code closely guarded until now—and aftercare practice, both fundamental and ultra-advanced, for both women and men.

Sage had me fast, and pray, and then she purified both the space and me; she worked me over, had me rest. Then three days later, she started mentoring, teaching, and training me in earnest—at a level she had never trained anyone else before. I was, she stated, the chosen one destined to learn and teach these life affirming insights.

She made me practice, over and over and over again until I had become intuitively masterful at it. "This is such a special, sacred practice that it should not be shared too easily."

Foremost amongst all of this, I was learning ever more about how to draw closer to God, how to discover your higher purpose, how to best communicate proactively, how to apologize in a healthy loving relationship, and how to live a more love, wellness and prosperity rich life.

Sage was well pleased. She told me that I was a great student, a worthy choice, and she knew I could and would help millions of couples become more aware, conscious, well-gratified and fulfilled. For the first time in my life, I understood the greater purpose that I was here for, and that was to not only use what I had learned to great effect in my own life, but to share this newfound wisdom and knowledge with the world. This was for the men ready to honor women, to nurture women, and to protect and provide for them. I now knew, without a

trace of doubt, that my future would involve dramatically helping the lives of so many others.

And as we spoke, I saw the desert etched in Sage's face, her heart, as she was in it. Solitude and hardship, home to frail hope, ancient memory. Worship and toil.

With memory, though, came sadness.

And always lurking in the doorway, in the corner of the room in the heat of the day, Shadow. Watching me, waiting for me to fall again. It was then that I knew that I must travel on, and soon.

My journey was not done. My time there grew too long.

So it was that early one morning she came to my smithy, leaning as she tended to do on the wall to watch me work for a while. That familiar gleam in her eyes held more sorrow that day, causing me to pause in my work.

"What troubles you, Sage?"

"It is time. You know this." And without any other explanation, I knew that she was right. My time in the oasis was simple, fulfilling. But it was a respite, a break from my soul's sojourn.

"I know, Sage, but I do not wish to leave."

"Such is life. Such is the journey you must endure and endeavor to see through. Do not despair. Your memory will live in my heart, as mine will in yours."

"Where must I go?" For I knew she would tell me the way.

"It is time for you to seek true solitude, to reflect on

all of the knowledge you have gained so far. It is time for you to sequester yourself. There is a cave to which you must travel. There you will face the spirit of the desert, your spirit. And your darkness."

She stooped low to the ground, waving me to join her. With the tip of one weathered finger, she drew five circles in the sand, interlocking.

"Your greatest struggle will be your life's great work. Your purpose. Our wounds become our guideposts to meaning." She pointed to the center circle. "Here lies the Infinite Source, the divine provider. Everything else is connected there. Down and to the right, are humanity's Wants, Needs, Desires. Meeting those impulses starts close to the center, working ever outward. See to those close by, expanding your field of influence. Not all of our Desires will be met. Ask the Creator which Wants are meant to be fulfilled."

HIGHER PURPOSE DISCOVERY

"As my mother always said, we serve Him by serving His people."

"Yes. Up and to the left, this circle represents our Gifts, our talents. They are a task to uniquely develop and employ. Then we must link our abilities to serving the needs of others. To the right, our enduring Passions reside. These things we pursue with all of our hearts, regardless of compensation. Temper your passions, for they give us meaning and fuel our efforts."

"And the bottom left?" I could not help but ask.

A sad smile crossed her features, a shadow of a cloud over the dunes. "Lifelong wounds, regrets. Here lies our greatest gifts if we work to overcome them."

"Lessons in suffering."

"Gifts from the Source. Our time here is meant to be spent struggling to be better. When we go deep, deep into this circle, the place which holds our own greatest fears, our greatest failures, our pain . . . there we can begin to heal."

And there I must face my Shadow.

The desert revealed my weakness. Forced me to move past my doubts and to open up to the needs of others by seeing my own needs. It showed me mercy, gifted me with a task, a passion in creating knives, fixing tools. That service employed my skill and my talent.

Still, I harbored grief. Resentment for the way life had used me.

Before the next sunrise, I set off. I prayed for hope. For strength.

But in my heart, I feared I would go to my death.

Stig's Journal, Day 61

For all of my days, I will not forget Sage's kindness, her vulnerability, grace, and honesty.

Relationships define our own needs as much as they involve the wants and needs of another. Not only in the case of lovers, soul mates, spouses, but even friends must consider how to navigate the maze of emotional interaction. Give and take.

At the core, communication is the foundation of any great relationship.

This comes in so many forms. Words, affection. In an intimate relationship, through sexual intercourse and physical touch, as well.

Sage told me that often, making passionate love is worth a year of counsel. Yet apologizing stands higher still.

Apologizing requires vulnerability. But it leads to deep intimacy.

First, you must ask if you need to apologize, if you are in the wrong. Check in with your friends, your spouse, your partner. Be vulnerable and allow them to be.

Exercise

Relationship Communication for Love, Clarity, & Appreciation

1. Beloved, my intention for us is to always love deeply, live fully, and contribute greatly together. What I absolutely love, adore, and appreciate most about you, especially . . . I appreciate how you . . . I cherish . . . I honor and hold dear

2. The main question that lingers in my mind and heart is . . .

3. Darling, Spirit willing, this month/week/day my intentions, plans and path includes . . . . . and please remain mindful of . . . . .

4. The vision, mission, dreams, hopes, top goals, and prayers I weave and pray for our shared future are . . . \

5. My Gracious Delightfulness, my heart yearns for us to . . .

Conflict Resolution

1. My love, when you . . .

2. It makes me feel . . .

3. The shadow projection I recognize here within myself is . . .

4. The judgment I carry is . . . And the story I make up as what that means is . . .

5. I am curious, would you be willing to . . .

6. Beloved, my heart's commitment to you is . . .

7. I just want to thank, honor and acknowledge you for . . .

8. I would love it if . . .

9. I am curious . . .

Chapter 10
The Cave and the Shadow

A man must get to a place where he can ask difficult questions. Of himself, and of the Universe. Reaching a level of desperation often precedes asking for assistance and advice.

What if it did not require such a dour situation to address our needs?

Sincerely surrendering your fears, worries, uncertainty, and your desire for healing is the first step. Put your fate in the hands of the Divine Source. Then you can move forward without the weight of carrying your burden alone.

Anyone who believes that their life is kept in control of a Supreme Being knows peace unlike any other. That's when they begin to see miracles and wonder in their life.

Find that place of solitude and silence to ask.

In surrender, we begin our Shadow work. Personal growth.

Work through your struggles, revisit the pain of an ordeal, the lessons you can learn from toil. This is the way to wisdom. Of moving beyond our wounds.

Silence sang once more, and I listened for a long time to my new companion. A day and a night passed traveling, accompanied by Crow and Coyote, but come the dawn of the second day, they fled as I neared the foreboding mountains.

Here, in the deepest heart of the Desert, they did not trespass.

For in that Wasteland, there was truly nothing. Only what I brought with me. My satchel, my thoughts, my aching soul.

Silence sat with me for two days, my lone companion. No spider, no scorpion, no serpent dared tread there. Sage was right, this is indeed isolation.

The first hours of my arrival saw me calm and meditative. As time passed, however, darkness multiplied around me. I knew they would. The bright sun held my deepest darkness at bay the first day. That strength sustained me through the cold night.

But by the end of the second, solitude scraped at my mental defenses. My inner voice resonated loudly by the end of that day.

So, I stilled that voice, tried to silence the turmoil within as without.

It worked, only that Shadow came to me that night, smothering me in the deepest black of the early hours. I woke choking, strangled and terrified, as if I were locked in a coffin.

He preyed on those fears.

Closing my nostrils, my mouth, my throat. So much was the torment that I ran from the cave, gasping, sobbing for any light whatsoever. The stars twinkled softly above, offering me a reprieve.

Sadly, the moon was faced away from my struggle. Each time I nodded off, I jerked awake, drenched in sweat. Something near a fever took me, though I know it was only an affliction of the mind affecting my body.

So, I sat alone in the dark for hours, staring at the figure in the recesses of the cave watching me. Waiting for me to sleep again.

His voice whispered and cackled, infusing every thought with fear and anger. Sadness, loss. Desperation.

"You will die out here. Alone. Forgotten."

"That does not scare me."

"Then why do you shake?" he hissed.

Trembling overtook me, the cold eating into me far worse than it should have. He was right. But not because I was afraid to die here in the desert. No, I was afraid of never having meant anything.

In that way, I was terrified.

"Only a fool would wander off into the desert. Or a man seeking his own death. Did your life merit such a waste? Do you not regret coming?"

"I do not, " I finally answered. "The challenge alone was worth it." I wish my voice sounded stronger, more convicted.

"Pride, pride. Always masking your true nature."

"And what nature is that?" I asked, trying to hide my bitterness.

"The facade of greatness. Cleverness, intelligence. Accomplishment. Wearing every achievement like a badge gleaming for approval and validation," Shadow taunted.

My mouth dried to the accusation.

This was not what I wanted. I wanted divine inspiration. Epiphany and the euphoria of self-discovery.

Instead, I faced the most trivial of my memories. Silly things, decisions and mistakes, embarrassments.

They piled on one another until they rose above me like a tidal wave. And then they changed color, shifting into hues of meaningless worry and sinking dread.

Had I learned anything? Had the things I learned mattered at all? Had the lessons I taught or the people who I met been of any consequence? Did I matter in their life?

Did my life matter?

Existential doubt crept into my very bones.

Was there even a God guiding my actions, listening to my pleas?

At some point, I slipped into slumber again. This time, Shadow did not wake me or assault me with panic. Instead, he infiltrated my dreams.

Pushing open the curtain, I stepped into the restaurant, smelling the rich aromas of meat and bread. My

stomach growled in anticipation, but more, I smiled at the opportunity to catch up with an old friend.

Yet when I saw him, he scowled at me.

"You are not welcome here any longer. You leech! All I have ever been to you is a favor asked and a promise owed. I see you for what you are, Stig."

"Please, my friend, my brother, let me explain–" "Get out. For we are friends no longer. We never were…"

Cast out, I stumbled in refuse in the alley, scrambling to find my footing. I tumbled deeper, the debris cascading down on my head.

In the dark, I fumbled down a long tunnel, a corridor lined with doors.

My parents, cousins, siblings, aunts and uncles, all closed their doors to my passing, turning away from me. Every eye accused me of failure, every mouth spoke of disappointment.

I left.

I ran away.

Now, I was no longer welcome to either family or friend.

A cry tore from my throat. Clawing toward the surface, I scraped at the mud, the dirt pouring into the hole I fought to escape. Reaching the rough stone of a desert cave floor, I woke again, shivering in the first light of dawn.

That light was precious, a balm.

But Shadow was not done with me yet, not even in the searing light of the day.

"Stig . . ." A sultry, buttery voice called to me, rousing me.

I stepped to the entrance of my cave, pushing my sweat-soaked hair from my face. The breeze did little to cool me. The woman walking toward me across the cracked landscape warmed me more.

She shimmered, her hands flowing around her, streams of sheer white and pale-yellow gliding. My heart leapt, my feet carrying me out to meet her. Yet I paused at the edge of the steppe, waiting to see if she would come closer.

Whatever was such a beauty doing here in this bleak place?

She was a flower, a blossom glowing in my eyes. "Your feet, they must be blistering. Come in, sit with me," I called to her. How unrefined I must look, shabby and unshaken. My clothes had long since faded, tattered in places.

But she looked at me with dark, liquid eyes, a sensual longing in that gaze drawing me toward her. She could answer my needs, assuage my loneliness.

Fantasies filled my mind, of long walks, conversations, holding hands.

The longer I gazed upon her, the more I longed for her. To rescue a stunning maiden of the sands, make her my own.

Logic cried to me that it was folly. The two of us, living in a cave?

With each step, she became ever more beautiful, a diffcrent aspect of my needs and wants. Glimmering ripples showed that she was water, a haze about her, cool air. She was so much more than love, she was desire, craving, hunger.

And she could quench my every need.

Such a thirst as I have never known nearly brought me to my knees, my tongue was parched, and my loins lusted for her. To feel her skin soft against mine, to drink from her well.

One step closer and I would run to her, give in to my aching heart.

The moment I moved to place my foot beyond the shadow of the cliff behind me, I hesitated. The sun was heading toward its zenith, its glare blinking. I looked down, noticing the fissure, the crack in the earth. Twenty feet down, jagged rock awaited me.

I nearly stepped in, headlong.

"Will you not join me and share this meal?" Her voice tugged at me. She smiled demurely, distracting me again, the edges of her lips curling up in deepest crimson. And her eyes, oh her eyes. Masked in black, those pools threatened to suck me in.

"You are welcome in my cave, to share a drink and a meal," I skirted, the heat of the day dragging at me.

"I do not wish to take your food from you, Stig. I

only came to offer you comfort. Sage sent me to you. For you." Her lithe hand was on my cheek, caressing it with scalding warmth.

Sensuality poured forth, her luscious scent, her smooth as silk skin.

I might have given in right then, if not for my past. Lust in my youth had led me astray, wounded my heart. Loving into a pit that never filled, only ever took from me.

Arms draped around me, bliss and contentment.

I knew it for what it was, misconceived emotions, hormones. Yet I was sorely tempted to lay my head on her chest, to rest.

It almost came as a surprise to find my hand gently pushing her away.

"My gracious lady, the simple fact that you came here to comfort me is comfort enough, and I thank you for keeping me in mind, your humble servant."

"But it is I that would serve you, master."

"I would be honored to wash your feet, feed you. Anything you might desire before sending you on your way." With each word, my voice grew more certain.

And that much more so when I saw her features contort in sneering rage. Disbelief.

"I thought you were a man, Stig!" she spat venomously. "The truth is that I knew the moment I saw you that you were nothing. You're weak. Pathetic. Impotent."

The last word struck at me at first, cutting deep,

tearing into my own insecurities and misgivings. My lack of a bride, never siring sons or daughters.

Shadows fluttered past me as she leered down on me, and I saw her for her true nature. This was another one of Shadow's ploys, an assault of a different kind.

"Peace, good lady. Be gone," I whispered softly, closing my eyes.

And just like that, she was gone.

Through the worst temperatures of the blazing afternoon heat, I at last found rest. Blessed, dreamless sleep. Another night. Another day.

A sound woke me in the middle of the night. Wheels, the clatter of wood drew me up and to my doorway in a hurry. My supplies were running low and any company would be welcome from a traveling merchant. News of the world, stories. Fire. Food.

Stepping from my sanctuary, warm light led me around a large stone. And there, sitting across a merry campfire, sat a jovial looking man, humming to himself. Jewels sparkled at his throat, his ears, his fingers.

This was a wealthy man, indeed.

"Good evening, I hope I did not startle you."

"Nonsense. I did not wish to disturb your slumber."

He grinned, inviting me with a wave of his hand to join him.

We spoke of great journeys, battles, legends. Through the late hours we sipped wine, ate the meat he cooked over the flames. Truly, he was charming, and I was starved for company. Surely, such a well-supplied fellow could afford to share.

We sang. We drank. And just before I dozed off, I reminded myself that I should offer to repay him in the morning, all the same.

Just before dawn, I startled awake, chilled to the bone.

Rising on stiff legs, I shuffled to my cave, wondering where the merchant had gone. Only to find my things strewn about. My supplies stolen or destroyed. My satchel torn, my food scattered. Even my boots were gone.

In my memory I saw clearly that the merchant's painted jewels were false, his tales all lies. The food he offered me was my own. How could I be so blind?

To be fooled so readily by a thief in the night. I knew only despair in those dark hours, and in my folly, I wept. Vulnerable and exposed, I did not hear the danger behind me until it was too late. I jerked to the side, a shock of pure instinct rushing through me as I heard the slithering of scales.

Just as the fangs of the viper sunk into my ankle, flooding my veins with venom.

I watched in horror, frozen by the agony in my blood as the creature turned to smoke, twisting into a man, grinning from ear to ear. Grinning as I began to shiver and sweat.

Grinning as he waited for me to die.

Stig's Journal, Day 66

Trapping darkness inside traps me in darkness.

I do not want to die. No one does. I do not want to suffer, to experience pain.

It is the only way to become stronger. Unless it kills me.

Survival in the wilderness teaches physical endurance. It also teaches will. Struggling in harsh conditions requires mental fortitude, emotional control. Our bodies fail when our mind gives up.

Conditioning builds stamina.

Spending time in self-reflection is the only way to know and test ourselves. Look within and examine the shadows, the darkness. How did they get there?

How can I process these feelings?

If I do not, they will lead to more suffering. More pain. The same mistakes, over and over.

Prayer

Where are my darkest shadows?

How are my wounds expressed in my actions?

How do they taint my decisions?

What aspects of my life are overshadowed by my darkness and pain?

In other people, what behaviors do I see that I dislike?

Why do I believe they act that way?

How is that reflected in my own actions? What do I admire about other people?

What do I admire about myself? What do I dislike about myself?

Is my dislike poisoning my attitude?

Can I forgive myself?

Part 3
Firewalk

Chapter 11
The Crucible

*T*learned hard lessons from the blood, sweat, and tears of living hard, traveling far, making many mistakes. Even more, I learned from great minds, speaking with generals, billionaires, world leaders and athletic champions. Doctors, pastors, priests, and healers.

Those meetings gifted me knowledge, but without context, without experience, using that knowledge cannot become wisdom. It cannot change our lives if we do not put it into practice.

Speaking to large crowds, sharing knowledge means nothing without earning the experiences yourself. Like a teacher instructing from theory instead of everyday use. That is the fire-walk. Living the knowledge we learn.

I have always been a hard learner. The Desert was a hard teacher.

Exhaustion shoved me from my nightmares. My body groaned; my joints inflamed. I was dehydrated, weak. But I was alive.

Dim rays leaked through the high gap in the stones, a window to the early morning sun in my abode. Even this early, a sliver of the golden fire across my arm left a shade of pink.

Slowly, I took stock of my physical state, my pain, my mental clarity. Then carefully, I sat up.

No punctures marked my skin. And the only hint that I had been attacked the night before were the scuffs of my own knees through the layer of dust on the stone floor.

That, and the length of rope coiled near the door. Some serpent.

A fit of laughter boiled up from deep within me, an absurd reaction, a rush of lightheadedness spinning my vision and driving me back down onto my back. Hysterics won out for a time, then I lay still, feeling somewhat relieved.

Silence returned when my laughter ceased.

Despite the fact that my voice offered some comfort, I needed Silence's more. She was neither oppressive, nor smothering. Simply a blanket to sooth me after my trials. For the rest of that day I sat on the stoop, fearful to wonder whether the worst of my ordeal was passed. Somewhere deep within, I knew there was more to come.

A sense of incompletion lingered.

I had faced down many of my fears, overcame Shadow's temptations and doubts. Only the wholeness that I

hoped still awaited kept me there without food and with a dwindling supply of water.

Sorting my things, I laid out what supplies remained. The bag was indeed torn, but most of the contents were merely spilled out. What cruel games Shadow played.

Well into the afternoon, my woes drifted on the tails of a nap, distant and vague. Hunger gnawed like a ravenous tiger and thirst sapped my strength. But these things hardly bothered me, I was becoming used to the sensations. Almost numb to them. What struck me awake an hour later, was a scent I had not smelled since entering the desert. Ozone wafted on the breeze, petrichor floating into my space. I could hardly believe it when a few moments later, I heard a tap, then a patter.

Rain. In the desert.

And not just a drizzle or a sprinkling. Huge drops plopped down, puffing clouds of dust. The first few vanished in a hiss of steam. Then the deluge began.

It came toward me, cheering louder than any crowd, a veritable roar compared to the absence of sound to which I had grown accustomed. The desert does nothing by halves. Why would rain be any different?

Thunder that had little to do with lightning echoed through my cave.

Huddling back against the wall, I reveled in the primal majesty of the downpour. Soon, water trickled down, a steady stream of clear crystal. Opening my mouth wide, I drank my fill in fits and bursts, careful not to overindulge.

Lightning flashed as darkness fell, showing me the state of the cave below my perch. The floor swam in a muddy pool, the water rising unreasonably fast.

Any thought of gathering water fled as the flood poured in above and below me, driving me higher, up onto a ledge. Already, my clothes and remaining gear soaked through. Shivers wracked my body as the temperature dropped.

Even high up in a corner of the cave, I could not find shelter from the wind and mist blasting through the cracks and gaps in the stone.

Hours felt like days, crouched in a nook, grasping my knees against my chest. Beneath me, the basin of the cave, my home for the past several days, frothed and churned as a murky, frigid river.

Another test, another night.

Sleep finds me sporadically, between bouts of shaking. By the time the sun rises and the water recedes, I am spent, curled as high up as I could get.

My eyes open, gritty and bleary.

Not a drop of water remained. Nothing to fill my canteen, the blistering sun glaring again as if to mock my suffering.

I eat a ration of what remains, sip my water.

The weather held, showing no signs of another storm, so I resumed my vigil, sitting in the shade of the cave's

doorway, looking out across the plateau. I pondered whether I should venture out, seek plant life, to hunt, to gather.

But as the day dragged on, the ground still humid, the Desert had another threat in mind for me. Almost in spite, in response to the barrage of rain, vermin came forth, swarming from the damp crevices in the rock, the sand. Fleas and flies assaulted me.

Spiders and scorpions sought higher ground, forced from their dens.

So, I was forced from mine for a time, trying to keep to the shade while avoiding the onslaught of biting midges and seething black gnats. Welts welled and stung all over my body, itching with fiery vengeance. As if by eluding the storm, I called the Desert's wrath down on me like a plague.

"If you are trying to teach me, your lessons are brutal," I muttered, gathering several cactus clusters on my way back to the cave. The worst heat of the day drove the insects away, but that also meant that I needed to go to ground or die of heatstroke.

That day I nearly left, giving up on everything I'd earned thus far.

Entering my cave, I flopped down, cursing my luck. Cursing the voice, I heard whispering to me again across the sands. Calling me to look deeper. Begging me to examine myself, to let go of my pride.

I ignored it in anger.

Near nightfall, I opened my bag to eat my last meal. Inside, I found only maggots. Mold. My head fell.

Where fury burned only a moment before, cold, hard bitterness festered. How could this happen? How could I let the last of my food get wet, become infested?

But I was at a loss. And out of energy.

I drank another ration of water and resolved to sleep away my despair. The morning certainly would bring new hope.

Until I rolled over in the early hours, my hand finding a small pool of water, already evaporating. Frantically, I snatched my waterskin, finding it under me, crushed. Split along the side.

Silence abandoned the cave as I screamed, shouted, beat my fists against the earth.

Nothing went to plan. I would fail in my journey, return to the oasis. If I could make it there with no food or water.

But even in my raging fit, I remembered that I was far from helpless. I knew where to look for honey, salt, and water. Before the sun rose, I stomped from my cave, scaling over cliffs and into ravines.

My single mindedness drove me forward, my anger fueling my refusal to concede. Nothing had stopped me so far. Serendipity, fate, or the Source had led me here. Had seen to my needs and kept me alive.

"I deserve to live, to thrive. To make it through the

desert!" I growled, digging along a rocky outcropping, my hands scraped and bleeding.

How foolish I must have sounded, if there had been anyone other than Shadow nipping at my heels. He skims along behind me, whispering bitter jeers and taunts at my back. Turning toward his casting mockery of my shape, I stomped him, kicked at him. And only succeeded in bursting the blisters on my feet inside my boots.

Pain compounded my delirium and frustration, and I nearly collapsed. I needed to return to the cave. However, when I rose and looked about, I did not know the way back. Windblown rock showed no footprints to retrace.

In every direction, stones and pillars of rock struck me as familiar, all of them the same. Cliffs and mountains peek at me over hills in every direction, all melding together like an unsolvable puzzle.

Stumbling out of a rift in the stone, I fell, tumbling down a slope back to loose, soft, searing sand. It was there, lying on the ground, staring up at the sky that I broke down. I cried, losing precious water.

And in that disoriented state, wallowing in self-pity, I completely missed the signs on the horizon. The pressure around me dropped. Silence gathered herself for a breath, then retreated.

Finally, I sat up, noticing a change. But it was too late.

Sweeping toward me across the land, a cloud of dune sand, sparkling glass, and wind bore down on me. It closed the distance in seconds, battering me and lashing at my skin and clothing.

In sheer panic I ran, groping ahead of me for any sign of shelter. Dirt blurs my vision, fills my nostrils and mouth. The wind tangled my loose clothing, binding my legs.

Falling hard, I dragged myself on until my arms gave out. I lay covering my head with my hands, flat on the ground, slowly flayed to death by nature.

And I thought, "This is where I will die."

Stig's Journal, Day 67

Fear lives only in the mirror.

Facing our mortality opens a door to a primal part of our souls.

My prayers continue as new desires and sometimes new temptations come to test me. All I can do is pray for God's protection, even from myself, not to sin. I may, but I hope and pray I will not. It is between me and Source and if I fail . . .

My desire is to be and do only good if I live another day. I take comfort in knowing there is forgiveness when I fall. I absolutely do not take it as a pass to sin. I must change, evolve.

I long to be a better person, for a better world. To obey, please and serve the Universe.

We are spiritual, infinite beings in a mortal body, here to have a human experience.

Prayer

What aspects of my life are not in harmony?

Where does conflict arise again and again? Are those conflicts a result of my errors?

How do my heart and mind work together? Are they at odds?

Or are their desires in sync?

Let me listen to my body, to hear the needs it has.

Show me the behaviors that compulsively surface for me that no longer serve my family, my community, and myself.

Chapter 12
The Earth Angels

S ince the beginning of time, humans have sought meaning. Looked to nature, to the stars, and within themselves.

Who am I? What is my purpose?

What if we are only here for one another?

We are Earth Angels. Every one of us, meant to minister and care for one another.

Vibrant agony whips across my back.

Every inch of my body screams as a trillion needles threaten to strip the flesh from my bones. Anguish cries out in my soul, "I should never have come to this place, I should have been grateful back at home."

Yet my heart raged against those thoughts, willing my journey to have meaning.

"If only I could just make it another moment," I thought. "To survive the sandstorm, this forge and crucible, and make my way back to the oasis. Then I would have at least been able to say I tried. Make an effort to try again."

I pictured a way out, some form of cover that might see me through.

Logic grappled with emotion, imagining such things would not make them come true. Doubt battered my will and my determination.

Until something else battered against my arm, stirring me from my cowering heap. To my right, I felt for the object, a fragment of wood. Just past it, another.

Following the trail of buried scraps, a silhouette manifested in the gloom, low and hulking. And as my hand came to rest on it, I touched the scoured wood of an old wagon, overturned and half submerged in sand.

It was almost as if I had dreamed the object in my mind, and willed it into existence.

Without a second thought, I wiggled through the gap between the wood and the earth, dragging myself into the protective shadow of the wagon bed. I breathed a sigh, although my instincts demanded that I check the enclosure for other occupants. Snakes might find such a relic a perfect spot to hole up.

Fortunately, no other creature occupied my shelter. Wood creaked, shuddering with the assault of the wind and dirt. Not a single hand hold or post offered me a chance to secure that haven to the ground. I could only pray that it would remain lodged in the dirt.

But I was safe for the time being, if a bit confined.

Until Shadow joined me in my refuge. He found his

way into my mind and heart. Fear of tight spaces began to tighten my chest. Then the darkness pressed in.

Outside, the storm raged.

Within me, another storm began. This time, there was no escaping it.

Regrets surfaced of every kind, tearing my hope to shreds. My own Shadow began to crush me into the ground. Scathing self-loathing, denial, and impotent anger welled up, boiled over.

Emotions that I longed to cast aside, things I believed I had mastered in myself so long ago. Shadow hung them on display, my immaturity, my pitiful lack of self-awareness.

"A real man would face the storm," he sneered, his grin an inch from my face. "A good man would not have needed to flee. You did them all a favor coming here to die."

"No… I will not die today."

"Then you will die tomorrow, or the next day, and no one will mourn your passing. All will have been for nothing."

"Not for nothing… I learned so much," I whispered, but my words fell flat.

His poison dulled my enthusiasm, diluting any positivity.

"Why do you bother, old man? You are not equal to this task. You are not equal to any great work."

The darkness of his abyss began to drag me in, a black hole of futility.

"You have. . ."

"I have—nothing left!" We sobbed as one voice.

My anguish rose above the sound of the tempest, reverberating back to me against the wall of the wagon bed.

"What have I found here? What did I think I would find but death? What answers can anyone find when everything else is stripped away?"

The words echoed out, mingling with the cacophony outside.

Shadow was still. Listening, watching me. Inside my mind, right behind my own eye lids.

"What more could I do? I came, I saw, I witnessed. I tried!" I shouted, crying out to the world, to the heavens, to the storm, to anyone who might care that I existed.

And most of all, I cried for mercy.

"Please . . . just show me what it is that I lack. What I need most . . ."

My heart split, spilling out my deepest secrets, my innermost thoughts, desires. Everything that I was poured forth, vomited out until I was completely hollow. And the Desert soaked it in, drank deep of my sorrow, my joy, my pain.

Silence rested her hand on mine.

The crackling torrent of the sandstorm grew distant to my ears, and I saw clearly my path to this point.

Leading all the way back to my home, my family, my youth, my birth. What was I meant for?

As if controlled by another, my mouth uttered into Silence, "Please, God, Spirit, Universe, whoever might be out there listening, I am undone. I am no more. I have given all I have. Is that enough?"

Moaning winds replied, humming against the shell of my safe haven. And in that soft song, I hear my own words echo back to me, "I came, I tried, I saw, I bore witness."

Then more, a grand retelling of my adventures.

"I met spirits and teachers along the way, Earth Angels, like Peddler and Sage. Coyote the Hunter, and Crow the Scout. Even Lion showed me the ways of the Maker, a higher power which created everything, including me. Every one of them was an emissary of the Source."

The voice speaking was my own, the story mine, as well.

But hearing it then, listening to my own accounting, I saw the truth in my actions from the start.

"I came here by choice. Not running away but running toward something. Every calamity I brought on myself was my own lesson to learn. Each mistake, pitfall, and folly, were solely my fault, my own doing."

And what had I done since I had come to this place? I mused.

I survived.

I overcame hardship.

I began to know myself, to know my limits and my strengths. I became accustomed to solitude, comfortable with my own presence and thoughts.

I faced tangible fears such as predators, starvation, thirst. And the intangible, the real fear that I did not like the man I was.

All throughout, my guide followed me on my path. My Shadow, who I only saw mocking, sneering, was in fact laughing at my denial because he was me. My spirit who wanted me to see the things that made me who I am, and accept them, reconcile them, or purge them to heal.

In Japan they say, "Without tears our soul cannot have a rainbow," and "Our tears speak for us as a prayer when we cannot."

Tears formed at my eyes; a laugh heaved in my chest. Tears of relief, of remorse and forgiveness, of fear and hope. Unrelenting determination formed around my will and my heart. All anchored to the acceptance that this storm was beyond my control, the world was beyond my control. But it is guided by loving hands.

So too, should my hands guide with purpose. Reaching out, I embraced my Shadow, and he clutched me in return, joining together as we were always meant to be, both the darkness and the light within me. Becoming whole.

The whisper, the song that called to me weeks, months ago, sang again.

Louder, more insistently.

"You are home, you are whole."

I opened my eyes to find the wagon had been flung away, ripped from the ground. Above me and all around me, violent wind and tinkling razor glass sand whirled. Yet not a fleck of sand touched me.

Because all around me, in a circle, my Earth Angels formed an impenetrable protective barrier.

Their spirits shimmered like mirages, like smoke in the breeze. The old woman smiled mischievously, the Mother of the Desert, the Desert herself.

And beside her, a traveler. Sometimes a Peddler, sometimes a Guide, sometimes a Storyteller.

A hunter, gatherer, the soul of instinct and natural order. Coyote stood secure in his place, content with his lot.

A young lion, a young man, a version of myself yearning to learn, to be a man, raised his face to the sky, the hope of an entire universe of possibilities written on his heart.

The Crow, wrapped in his cloak of feathers, smirking at the shock on my face. Always looking at me with just one eye, the other on the horizon, looking for signs and symbols. His was the future, the path ahead.

Winds raged for hours more, raining sand down until the land became unrecognizable. Through it all, they stood watch over me, protecting, showing me what I should be for others.

Finally, the storm slowed, moving away.

My guardians faded as the sun broke through the haze, but they remained in my heart. I took my first step from the circle, exhausted. But whole.

Stig's Journal, Day 68

I am as I have always been, completely different.

Harmony. Balance. These things come from managing our lives. Working with ourselves and those around us to create an ecosystem in which to reside. Whether or not we thrive is up to the conditions of the situation and how prepared we are to deal with them.

I created a harsh environment for myself by going to the desert. Much in the way I fought within myself before I left home, creating an inhospitable place to live. But we cannot stop living within ourselves.

We can change our environments. So too, we must change our internal environment. This way we can serve as a beacon of security and guidance for others.

Prayer

Have I refused to heal?

What have my preciously held issues and grudges cost me?

Who are they hurting and how?

Show me which factors of my person need to be adjusted, which ones are damaged.

Let me be receptive to change and acceptance.

If I don't, and stay on this path, where will it lead me? What consequences will my bitterness or anger cause?

What will it cost me to let go and allow myself to transform?

Chapter 13
The Way Home

Write down what you believe is your greatest genetic gift. Something that comes naturally. Now write down what you worked impossibly hard to attain. Which one brings more joy and satisfaction?

They are very distinct things. What we can do, and what we strive to do.

A bulldog cannot become a greyhound. They are both for different purposes.

Finding our way to a state of contentment starts within. Accepting the things we have and honing them, taking the things we desire to excel at and adding them to our person. Life is much more fluid when we zero in on that which comes naturally.

This is the way we move forward, the way we shape a space for ourselves in the world. This is the way home. The dregs of the storm stuttered, rumbling away across the expanse in the distance.

I stood still for a time, letting the dust settle, my tense muscles loosening. Walking slowly, I beheld the landscape around me, stark, smooth, and bleak.

It was as if the hand of God scoured the world clean all around me, and I felt that same sense of cleansing deep within my being.

Spats of tiny cyclones twisted nearby, but I feared them not.

Soft sand sifted underfoot, cushioning my steps as I checked the position of the sun, took note of my surroundings. Though I did not precisely know my location, I remembered how to get my bearings, and calm blanketed my thoughts like the golden dunes all about me.

Clouds speckled the sky, providing the mercy of shade from the sun.

Each detail I noted in my mind, more present then than I had ever been before. Heat rippled up from the ground, baked the air still, but I was inured to it. I was a part of the desert, now.

And it was a part of me.

Carefully crisscrossing up the back of a long slope, I made my way toward higher ground. Choosing a direction would be instrumental in my finding water and shelter for the night. In the long run, my path would necessitate my returning to the oasis for supplies before moving on.

Which was what I intended to do next. My time in the scrapyard was precious to me. Iconic and defining. But it was done.

Just as I crested the rise, I caught a flash of black in the sky.

"Crow! Good to see you, my friend."

"I'd say the same if you were much to look at!" Crow cawed down to me, circling.

"He is just masking his worry. The wretched creature was fussing and fretting for days looking for you," Coyote panted, appearing next to me as shades of orange colored the horizon.

"I fear that I may have gone a bit astray," I chuckled, scanning the rocky hillocks all around me. This part of the desert looked almost familiar, but then, it all did.

"You fear no longer, though." The Coyote sniffed, as if he could sense the change in me. "Will you hunt with me one last time this night?"

"Nothing would make me happier, my old companion." But I felt a hesitance in that decision, an insistence that I needed to get moving toward my destination.

"Go," he murmured, seemingly indifferent, "There will always be a trail to follow, and your hunt lies elsewhere. Such is the way of the Wastes."

"Thank you, Teacher."

Coyote shook himself, trotting off to his nightly hunt. He did not say goodbye, merely glancing back over his shoulder with a flap of his ears. Then he was gone.

"So too, must I go. Crow, which way?" I asked.

"Still depending on me to do all the hard work, eh?" Crow quipped.

"If only you knew how?"

"The Desert scoured what little brain you had left." Crow taunted.

"Then I must rely on the talents of others to shine where they are needed," I agreed.

"And I will rely on you to feed me, then," he said.

I laughed, following along his course. No sooner did we skirt the base of another dune, that I heard familiar sound, the jingle of a bridle and the rattle of wagon wheels. Just around the bend, he wobbled to a stop, puffing on a pipe as he watched me approach.

"Stig, my boy! What a chance encounter."

"I am not sure I believe anything is left to chance." I grinned up at Peddler, raising an eyebrow.

"Then how do you explain this? I was riding along, minding my own business when an old, broken wagon fell from the sky! Landed right next to me, scared my team half to death," Peddler said.

"It sounds like the Spirits were looking out for you."

"Or warning me that I am getting old and need to stop taking risks crossing the desert!" He laughed, leaning back on his bench.

"Perhaps both of our time here is at an end," I mused, stretching and looking about. The close of the day melted into stunning pinks and purples.

"If you are ready," he said, his eyes smiling.

"What do you think, Peddler? Am I? What does the Wise Man of the Desert see when he looks upon me?"

"Wise Man, Stig. We all don different coats throughout our journeys. I have seen you wear many, in a short time."

"Wise words. But not an answer," I replied.

"But what answer could I give that you cannot find in yourself? And what are wise words, compared to a drink of water?" His face beamed as he casually offered me his canteen. I took it, sipping the clear liquid, breathing a sigh of relief.

Peddler waved to me to join him on the bench. "Where are you headed? I would offer you a ride, at least for a while. You look like you might be a bit tired." A gleam in his eyes told me that he knew much more than he let on.

Laughter erupted from me and I tossed my head back, opening my arms and my heart wide. I let joy fill me, enjoying the moment.

"I appreciate the offer, but I must decline. You see, my path lies before me, and I must heed that call."

Peddler nodded, tossing me a pack from his wagon, filled with supplies. "Our meeting was a gift, and I hope we will again."

"I have faith that we will. Someday, on a long-forgotten road."

"Only if you forget yourself again. Until you become

a Wise Man in your own right. Where, pray tell, does your path lead now?" Peddler asked.

"Why, just over the next hill, my friend." I wagged my eyebrows at him, sharing in his mirth.

"If I might offer a boon . . ."

"I always welcome your advice," I said.

"Try that one, there." He pointed toward the rugged incline in the distance. When I turned back to thank him, he was gone.

I scaled the hill.

The song of the Desert followed me, pushing me forward where before it pulled at me. She kept rhythm with my steps, pacing along with my breath, conserving water and energy.

When I reached the summit, I looked up, somehow knowing exactly what I would see there.

My home on the horizon, my city.

Only now it welcomed me, beckoned me with great purpose.

Stig's Journal, Day 69

I shall miss the desert.

Someday, I will return. In the meantime, I will remember, bring my journey to mind and think on it often. I continue on my path, thinking most about the people I met here: the Earth Angels who changed my life forever.

Finding a bounty of fulfillment with nothing is my biggest takeaway. Discovering a spirit of gratitude, mastering the art of being thankful is my greatest gift from that time.

We are all here to help restore the world to wholeness, to love deeply, to live fully, and to contribute greatly.

My discovery of self will guide me. Better people create a better future, a better world. To create better people, we must invest in one another.

Prayer

Show me how to give back. Who needs my help?

Sustain in me a charitable spirit. This is how we will prosper.

Giving and receiving.

How do I feel at the end of this step in my journey?

Where will I go next?

Let me rest in the meantime, to replenish my energy, to digest life's lessons.

Guide me to my highest self.

Epilogue
Called to a New Purpose

e are quick to forget. When we do, we must only do two things to begin again:

Simplify.

Return to Source.

I came home with my head held high, but ready to face the future with an eagerness only known by an awakened soul.

Humility, dedication, and determination would be my anchors. The people whom I cared for deserved nothing less.

Only in this manner would I start to heal any wrongs I left in my wake. In myself, in those around me.

In my absence, the worst uncertainties of the pandemic had passed. I wasn't the only one trying to establish a new normal. The world at large had gone through a reset, never again to return to certain old paradigms.

It seemed people were demanding new levels of truth and transparency in everything, even in the ways they expressed their life and their work. Many were seeking new ways of being. The Holy Spirit continued whispering, "This is what I prepared you for."

I felt love embrace me everywhere I looked.

When I re-entered society, I knew my purpose. To serve each and every person I could using the lessons and the sacred secrets I'd learned in the Desert. In the Desert I had found the clarity of my calling.

I heard God say to me, "You have proven your love for Me, you have endured your ordeal well. You know extreme thirst, hunger, and loneliness, and you are now ready with compassion and wisdom to take your water to where the thirsty are. Go meet them in their darkness and offer them your empathy and wisdom. Help the lonely, the spiritually weakened, and the sexually wounded. Show them the path to a new, better, eternal life and how to discover their higher purpose revealed."

I was now ready to be the man I was always meant to be.

Stig's Journal, Final Entry, (for now):

I will have faith. I will trust. I will choose life.

I have gifts and a purpose. My contribution to the world matters. We all matter in the great plan.

Let us use our gifts for the purpose they were given.

Make the most of your potential, do not waste it. Go help people. Spread love and hope. Someone needs you.

This will be our legacy. The lives we change and bless.

Part 4
Gratitude, Affirmations, and Prayers

Gratitude

Thank You for life.

I need you. I love you and need you in my life. Thank you for saving my soul. You know my dark side and yet you live and bless me. Help me. Cleanse me. I want to serve you with a pure heart.

Thank You for all you have already done for me, and shown me. Thank You for the destiny partners you have brought into my life, and the ones still coming now.

Thank You for my talents, my bountiful opportunities, and your abundant provision in my life.

Thank You for my trials in The Valley Of Death.

Thank You for sending your Earth Angels to me, and allowing me to become one to others.

Thank You for your miracles.

Affirmations

The Divine Source loves me. The Universe, God, the Spirit of life is the unlimited, endless provider of all that I need and more.

Glory to the Provider for my love, health, professional success and prosperity.

I am blessed. I am alive.

I am worthy of forgiveness, success, growth, grace, and wellness.

Life happens for me, not to me, and it is magnificent.

Today is the day of attraction, miracles, wonder, and manifestation.

Everything I need will come to me in good time. I must ask for it. Seek it. Take it.

I am good, my gifts benefit those around me.

Prayers

May the will of the One be done today.
May I follow the path laid out for me.

Take my gifts and use them. Show me where I am needed.

Let me serve You. Let me serve your children. May I reach
out and help as many as I am able.

Allow me to be a bridge to You.

Show me the gift of Spiritual Manifestation.

Let me share the bounty of my success.

Reveal Your wonders to me and open my eyes to see when
suffering blesses me with guidance.

Open the floodgates of true love, real health, world class
creativity and innovation, and great prosperity for me now.

Let my will be one with the will of the Creator,
the great Teacher.

Spirit Whispers
The Experience

Imagine joining David (Stig) in the desert, or in Spain, France or Italy or elsewhere for your own guided spiritual vision quest, and a deep dive shared educational adventure led by David and others with him sharing the real story behind the story, teaching in greater depth what is here, and going far beyond.

David also offers individual private client mentorship and coaching; and is selectively available as a speaker, trainer, and fire walk authority for culture and team building in the domains of leadership, sales, and personal development.

His partner and he also offer sophisticated, respectful and sizzling hot workshops on how to manifest your dream partner, on relationships communication, romantic-erotic-sacred sexuality and the three most important things to do to maximize your chances of making your partner obsessed with you and for them to be totally loyal and faithful and never want to leave or lose you.

He also certifies coaches in his proprietary Core 9 System—the world's most advanced and comprehensive personal development system. He focuses on the spiritual, the physical, the financial, and sexual integration, balance, and harmony in your life.

Become eligible for membership in his Global Entrepreneurs Group made up of dynamic entrepreneurs, successful professionals, private equity investors, and other fabulous people.

To contact David: 702-483-7002
Please visit my website: spiritwhispersofficial.com

About David Fabricius

David Fabricius has been described as a perfect fusion of James Bond and Indiana Jones with a heart of Gandhi—capable, proficient, elegant, rugged, compassionate, and wise.

David grew up barefoot in Africa where he volunteered for and went through Army Special Forces training. He worked as a respected instructor in an elite special operations unit specializing in hostage rescue.

Over the years he has earned numerous awards locally and internationally for personal excellence, entrepreneurship, public speaking, community building, and selfless service to humanity.

David is a world-renowned business and inspirational speaker, leadership development, and sales trainer, as well as a culture builder for elite groups and Fortune 500 companies and corporations globally across six continents.

He is a global authority in fire walking as a powerful team-building experience for breakthrough and unification. He inspires greatness and helps organizations set new all-time sales records. He excels at building a winning culture that brings better results faster in more sustainable ways.

His popular Fire & Ice experience is epic and one of the most highly rated transformational events globally today! It is extremely popular with the world's leading organizations for business leaders.

David is the founder of The Global Entrepreneurs Group. The members include dynamic entrepreneurs, successful professionals, private equity investors, as well as other fabulous and extraordinary people committed to redefine world class excellence, raise the standards of greatness in America, and help to make the world a better place for all.

He teaches ancient sacred wisdom techniques to women's groups, couples, and individuals. Additionally,

he helps men and women to discover their spiritual purpose, communicate better within relationships and make sex more romantic, erotic and most importantly facilitate sacred, healing and nurturing.

David also leads men's initiation adventures emphasizing healthy masculinity and spirituality to help them become better leaders, providers, and protectors.

David Fabricius is Mr. Not Just Words: he is the choice of discerning and distinguished decision-makers worldwide.

David has shared stages and spent time rubbing shoulders backstage and on the streets of Las Vegas, Rome and far beyond with Mark Victor Hansen, Robert Kiyosaki, Mark Wahlberg, John Travolta, Mel Gibson, Dr. Jordan Peterson and with rock stars like Gene Simmons and many more. He has been featured in well over 400 media outlets globally including the BBC world news. His clients include Microsoft, Mass Mutual, Motorola, Lucent Technologies, EO, IMD Switzerland and the head of their Swiss Private Bank have attended his teachings and many more. His work is endorsed by billionaires, retired American Special Forces leaders and the captains of industry worldwide.

David loves travel, dogs, yachts, photography, art, classical music, country living, and Italian food.